CINEPHILIA

A Novel by Grant Jolly

MANIC RAVEN PRESS

Cinephilia © 2018 Grant Jolly

First published in paperback by
MANIC RAVEN PRESS © 2018

1

The moral right of Grant Jolly to be
identified as the author of this work has been
asserted in accordance with the Copyright,
Designs, and Patents act, 1988.

ISBN: 978-1-9999629-1-3

MANIC RAVEN PRESS

For my dear friend, Moira Macdonald. Thanks for having faith in my rambling mind. I also want to dedicate this book to my friend, Harry Stewart. You are my biggest fan, rock a great beard, and have always encouraged me to chase the dream.

FOREWORD

by Rania M. M. Watts

"Love, love changes everything
Hands and faces, earth and sky.
Love, love changes everything
How you live and how you die.
Love can make the summer fly,
Or a night seem like a lifetime.
Yes, love, love changes everything,
Now I tremble at your name.
Nothing in the world will ever be the same."

Love Changes Everything
by lyricists Don Black & Charles Hart

I've never written a foreword before – other than the one for my third book, *Cockroach Blueprint: 101 Ways To kill A Cockroach.* But that was more of an instructional. This is brand new territory for me. Please bear with me as I stumble through my first.

I found *Cinephilia* to be a surprisingly honest read. At times it reminded me of scenes from

Dexter, Breakfast at Tiffany's, and *Donnie Darko.* I'll explain all those references as I get further into this foreword, as well as the reason I quoted *Love Changes Everything,* from the Andrew Lloyd musical, *Aspects of Love.*

I would recommend this book to anyone who is interested in reading something pure. *Cinephilia* is filled with raw emotion. The story ensconces all the wonderful letters and symbols we look for in a book, and can stand on its own two feet without any aid.

Firstly, let's start with the title, and why the theme of love is so predominant throughout this read. There are various types of love. When I was growing up, I could not get enough of the cinema – it was a genuine love affair. Never did I realise in my wildest dreams, or even contemplate for one moment, that a word like 'cinephilia' existed. But it does. And it does indeed mean a love of cinema—is that not the coolest thing ever? So, you see, there is love present, even in the title.

The first reference I mentioned was *Breakfast at Tiffany's.* There is a scene in the second chapter of *Cinephilia* that reminds me of the emotion behind the phrases, where the main character has a cat and the affection he showers over it. This reminded me of the scene from *Breakfast at Tiffany's* where Audrey Hepburn tells her cat to 'scram' – releasing the little cat to the wilds of the nasty streets of New

York City. A kind of thought if you could make it here, you can make it anywhere – when she takes the cat out of the car.

When she realises what she has done, she searches for the cat. What happened next reminded me of the scene from *Cinephilia*, where all the affection in the world is showered over Luna. That type of expression is what I found to be extremely relatable. When Audrey Hepburn realised what she had done and went in search of this poor, lonely, and scared cat who had no idea what was going on, she scooped him up and showered him with love. As human beings we constantly question ourselves and our purpose, and sometimes we see things through the eyes of animals and don't appreciate what that means for us, exactly.

Throughout the pages of *Cinephilia* there is, of course, not a scary bunny like in *Donnie Darko*, but a creepy goat that keeps rearing it's ugly head throughout nightmares – it's totally relentless the way that it comes after our protagonist, Freddy Moon, instils the fear of whatever god one believes in—or not.

The *Dexter* reference – let's say things get a little more than bloody when our main character finds his mum in a not-so-flattering manner. This reminded me of the start of *Dexter,* where he was found in a storage locker, saturated in nothing but crimson blood. I can't imagine a million years over what kind of impact that would have on a child, to be the one to find their mum like that.

Finally, I added the lyrics of *Love Changes Everything* to this foreword, because love is such a predominant theme throughout. Love is truly the one thing that has the power to change even a depressed loner like Freddy Moon.

Now that has been established, there are also aspects of romantic love, self-love, self-loathing, and the pain of constantly second-guessing one's self. All these emotions are present throughout.

Cinephilia reads like a frenetic anxiety attack, open to various imaginations. There is so much to take away from the story—if you let the virus take hold.

— Rania M. M. Watts

SUICIDAL TENDENCIES

Loneliness has followed me my whole life, everywhere. In bars, in cars, sidewalks, stores, everywhere. There's no escape. I'm God's lonely man.

Travis Bickle,
Taxi Driver

LOVE IS A HOWLING BITCH FROM HELL. Love drives us all mad. Love makes us do the craziest things. Things we would never normally dream of doing. My name is Freddy Moon, and I think I may be completely insane.

I had done it. I had finally done it. I didn't even feel bad – not a single shred of remorse in my body. Instead, a strange calmness washed over me like I had reached a state of nirvana. I had found a new drug. A drug better than anything I'd ever experienced in my life. An unprescribed elixir. I was addicted.

For you to understand, I will go back to the

beginning. Back to where the roots first took hold of my heart.

It was on a Tuesday night in the middle of August, 2012. The world was furious, grey, and weeping. If I close my eyes now, I can still hear the rain dancing down the gutter, and the sound of the drops exploding on the metal bin in my back garden.

On that night, in the middle of August, I had decided I was going to take my own life. Why? I was tired of fighting the demons in my head, of being alone, having no friends, and no family. I was mentally exhausted.

At twenty-six years of age, I was terrified of growing old, fading away to nothing, unnoticed. I worried a lot back then about how they would find my decaying body, and how long it would take someone to find me in the first place.

Suicide was in my genes. My only way out. my eject button. I was destined to die alone in a blaze of cheap whiskey and cigarettes. My mother had turned out the lights in a similar fashion when I was the tender age of twelve.

I had been to Cub Scouts. I found her lying there when I got home, face down on the green speckled carpet in our living room, with an abundance of multicoloured pills scattered everywhere. She was holding a burnt-out cigarette in one hand, a bottle of vodka in the other, and there was puke around her mouth. I may have been young but I could still tell she was gone.

I didn't cry. I got on my knees, told her I loved her, kissed her on the head, then dialled 999. My mother was pronounced dead at the scene on January 21st, 1998.

Titanic was released to the world two days later – the first film I ever experienced on the big screen. The week before her death, my mum promised to take me, buy me popcorn and a Slush Puppy, but I watched it alone. I hadn't saved enough pocket money for the popcorn—or the Slush Puppy.

My mum divorced my dad eight months before. I guess you could say I lost them both in the same year. I haven't heard from my dad since the divorce, not even a phone call. He could also now be dead. All I knew for certain, in those dark times, is that I was lost with no moral compass.

Anyway, you get the idea. My time was up. *It's better to burn out than to fade away.*

As a sufferer of manic depression and anxiety, it wasn't hard to find the pills for the job. I had to make sure I done it right. The last thing I wanted was to wake up as a vegetable in the morning, dribbling all over the place, incapable of having another shot at topping myself correctly.

I crushed up fifty-six mirtazapine, twenty-four sertraline, and sixteen codeine pills, added a couple of diazepam to the mix for good measure, and scooped the pile of powder into a pint glass with the side of my hand. I half-filled the glass with some cheap whiskey I bought from Asda earlier in the day. (Highland Earl understood my predicament.)

The liquid bubbled for a minute or two and formed a frothy head before settling. I took the glass with me to the living room, set it on the coffee table, sat on the sofa, and lit a cigarette.

I wanted to watch my favourite movie, one last time, before fading away. *Taxi Driver* has always been my most treasured piece of cinematic art. The film was made by, who I perceive to be, the best director in the world, and was written by my favourite screenwriter. Even the casting is perfect – a handful of phenomenal actors grace the screen with raw, believable emotions. That doesn't come along too often, especially not these days.

I could relate to Travis Bickle; I agreed with his views on life. He was right, even back in the seventies, the world was full of scum. I want an apocalyptic rain to fall and clear them all away, purifying the air I breathe into my blackened lungs.

A FRIEND IN NEED
IS A FRIEND INDEED

I slid the DVD into the player and smiled as the score kicked in. *Splendid choice of exit music.* I sat back on the sofa and took a swig of the cocktail – it tasted like Imperial Leather soap.

I was about to take another brave gulp of the self-manufactured poison, but a strange noise stopped me in my tracks. I walked over to the DVD player, hit *Pause*, and stood for a moment. *There it is again,* I thought – a frantic scraping in my ears.

There was a gut-curdling squeal. It sounded like an injured child—but it was after 11:00PM and all the kids had retired from riding their bikes for the night. I went to investigate.

I followed the scraping and it led me down the hallway, through the kitchen, to the back door of my house. I turned the key and opened the door. As soon as there was a gap, a red and white ball darted by my feet. I slammed the door and gave chase.

I was cautious as I entered the living room. *What's in there?* A fox was my first guess – foxes are forever rummaging through the bins and making a mess.

I was shocked to find a fat cat cowering with fear

on my sofa. The poor thing was soaked to the bone, covered in blood, and shivering to the core.

'Hey, it's okay.' I said.

I stretched my hands out in a gradual manner, reassuring the injured cat. She looked up at me with glazed-over eyes as I edged my way towards her. She was too exhausted to run away. She couldn't, even if she tried – sprinting through the house had likely been her final burst of energy.

I rushed to the kitchen to fetch a first aid kit, a basin of warm water, and a cotton flannel. I sat next to the cat on the sofa, spent a few minutes gaining her trust, then inspected the obvious injuries.

'What have you been up to? Did you get yourself into a fight?'

She was terrified, in pain, and confused.

'I know how you feel,' I said. 'I'm all alone too.'

The cat was young – not much older than a kitten – and I felt sorry for her. The injuries were not as bad as I first thought they were. There seemed to be more blood than there actually was, vivid like paint on her brilliant white fur. After cleaning the cuts and grazes, I wrapped the cat in a blanket, and she fell asleep on my lap.

DIVINE INTERVENTION

I looked at the glass on the table and had a moment of clarity. *How could I end it when there was a defenceless animal in need of my help?* The cat needed me and, if I'm honest, I needed her.

She entered my life at just the right time – one hour later, maybe less, and there would have been a different ending to this story. Fate was at play. Divine intervention like in *Pulp Fiction*. A stupid cat had saved my life. The funny thing is, I despised cats until that night.

I named her Luna, for she was a mystery to me, just like the midnight disco ball hanging in the sky.

I pressed *Play* and transported my mind to the streets of New York City with Travis.

WEDNESDAY MORNING

I fell asleep on the sofa. When I opened my eyes in the morning, a big set of marble-blue eyes were staring back at me. Luna was purring and I could tell she was hungry. I nudged her from my lap and got to my feet. She followed closely behind as I made my way into the kitchen, occasionally brushing up against my legs, her bushy tail pointing to the ceiling the whole time.

I had a look in the cupboards to see if I could find anything for the cat's breakfast. By chance, I found two cans of tuna. I grabbed a plate and a bowl. Luna purred louder as I opened the cans, pacing around with vigour at my feet. I put the tuna on the plate and placed it next to her on the floor – she devoured every flake. I poured some milk into the bowl, set it down, and she lapped it up.

I was empty inside and didn't feel much of anything, but taking care of Luna and watching her fill her belly warmed my heart.

Am I a terrible person for wanting to keep you? What if there's some heartbroken kid strolling around crying, worried sick about his beloved cat? Shouldn't I be putting up MISSING CAT flyers?

She never had a collar. The cat was a stray. I told myself that anyway. Now that I had named her, she was my new companion. And if I'm entirely honest, I never had any intention of giving her back in the first place, even if she did have a family out there looking for her.

I looked up at the clock on the kitchen wall, 8:16AM. I didn't want to get ready but I had work in forty-four minutes – The Troll had been on my ass all week for being late. My guts were aching. I figured it was anxiety; my brow was sweating and my skin was burning up like it always did when I was edgy. The stuff I was drinking the previous night – even if I did only have one sip – may have had something to do with it. Either way, it was time to get a move on. I had a quick shower, brushed my teeth, got dressed, closed all the windows, said goodbye to Luna, and left for work.

THE OLD MOTION PICTURES

I was a projectionist at my local cinema. I won't name the place. If you've been there before you'll know which one I'm talking about. Let's call it...The Box, just for the sake of this story. I had worked there for almost three years and it was the only thing in my life worth waking up for.

I once dreamed of being a writer. I even went to university to study film and English literature, but it was only ever a fantasy. Anyway, I enjoyed being a projectionist; it's people like me who keep the old motion pictures rolling. That was my motto. In reality, advancing digital technology was creeping up on me. My days would soon be numbered – the future stealing away my present, my here and now, right from under my feet like some bloodthirsty shark circling the depths of the ocean, waiting patiently for me to submerge.

I couldn't find a parking space when I arrived at work. If inconsiderate people didn't park like total morons, I would have no problem finding one. Drivers that park in the middle of two spaces get my blood boiling. I was five minutes late by the time I found a big enough space for my Jeep.

I ran across the road, dashed in through the automatic doors with my head down, hoping I could speed past the office without being noticed by The Troll on my way in.

I have always enjoyed the experience of walking into a cinema. The first thing I notice is the smell. Popcorn is the dominating flavour in the air, then comes the sticky sweetness of soft drinks, the scent of sizzling hot dogs. And then, if you concentrate hard and focus your nostrils, the undertones of vomit take hold. Some fat kid – devouring their way to chronic obesity – is always the culprit.

The aroma is just a part of it. The dazzling fluorescent lights suck you in. The film posters sell escapism. *Step in, step in,* they persuade you. *C'mon in here and escape from the real world for two hours.* In all fairness, it was a great way to escape the gloom of real life for a while.

The Box was my cinema of choice, even before I started working there – it was the first cinema I had ever visited. The place where I sat alone for two hours in awe, DiCaprio owning the screen like a fucking god in *Titanic*. My mouth dry, struggling to breathe with the sheer astonishment of what I was witnessing—the most gigantic film presentation in the world, flashing before my curious eyes.

I hurried along the burgundy carpet, up the four stairs at the entrance, and across the foyer to the locker rooms – a trail of spilled popcorn crunching underfoot with every step. I placed my backpack in the locker, picked up my name badge, pinned it to my shirt, closed the locker, hurried back along the foyer, and chapped on the manager's office door to get the schedule for the day.

RUMOUR HAS IT

My manager, Angus, was mostly okay with me. He was a balding, forty-something year old guy with a wife and kids. A few creepy rumours surrounded him, and some of the stories were alarming, to say the least.

There was once a rumour that he slept with an eighteen year old student – she was doing weekend shifts at the time to make some extra cash while studying – and she fell pregnant. Old Angus was less than pleased when he found out she was carrying his child, so he forced the girl to get an abortion, offered her a full-time job, and paid her £200 to keep her mouth shut.

This happened before I was employed by The Box. I was sceptical when I first heard the story, but there *was* something a bit off about Angus. I couldn't put my finger on it—he was too straight-edged. I thought about that story a lot and it made me uncomfortable.

If the abortion story was true, what else had he done? Was he a pleasant exterior with a dark heart? Time would tell. People like Angus have a way of slipping up and getting caught, usually because they lose track of their own lies.

There was no answer. I knocked on the door again. I was eager to get on with my shift, finish up, and get back home to check on Luna. *I need to buy cat food. Maybe I could get her a nice new collar.* I thought as I stood there waiting.

THE TROLL

Each day when I knocked on the manager's door, it could go one of three ways. One: Angus answers. He doesn't give me too much of a hard time for being late. He does, however, make me suffer one of his terrible jokes that drag on forever. I smile but I'm dying on the inside – there's only so long you can hold a fake smile before it begins to look like you're constipated.

The second outcome: The Troll answers. I need to look at her fat, red, bespectacled face. The Troll was the assistant manager. Her real name was Erin. The name Erin reminds me of Julia Roberts, when she played the lead role in *Erin Brockovich*. Julia Roberts is naturally beautiful – The Troll resembles a much smaller version of Miss Trunchbull from *Matilda*. Even her attitude was the same.

The Troll taps her pink Casio watch with her chubby index finger as she complains about me being late. Her voice becomes silent and her chops begin to move in slow motion as she rambles on. I fantasise about forcing my fingers through the lenses in her glasses, gouging my nails through her eyes, and into the back of her nasty skull. When I snap back I nod and agree with her, even though I don't catch a single word. It's all bullshit.

The third outcome: Karen, the supervisor, answers the door. This was always my favourite outcome and only happened about once a week, if I was lucky. Karen is petite, well spoken, and has a smile to die for. She has a plain Jane look about her. I like that. Her lips are pale, pink, and plump. I mainly fantasised over what it would be like to fuck Karen – she was the girl I often thought about when masturbating – but she's also a good laugh and never mentions the fact that I'm sometimes late. Karen has a boyfriend called Dave. I'm pretty sure he's a homosexual, but that's none of my business.

ENTER THE TROLL

The door opened. I looked down and there she was, The Troll. All four foot of her. Her hair scraped back in a greasy bun. My eyes focus in on the dry flakes of dead skin resting on her noggin. I'm sure I can see something moving around under there. *Is there a fist full of maggots squirming from the heat under that bun? Or am I just imagining things?*

'Late again, Freddy, late again. How hard is it to get here on time?'

Her fat chops wobble like jelly, igniting a flashback to school dinners and that one time I found a lump of tissue paper trapped inside my lemon dessert.

Go on a diet and have a bath.

'Sorry, I've not been feeling myself recently, see?'

I wiped the sweat from my brow and lowered my hand. Erin looked at the sweat streaked across my palm.

'Don't be disgusting.'

'Just for the record, I can never find a parking space out there. People park like complete idiots.'

'Right, enough of the excuses for one day, eh? Just try and sort yourself out. You're replaceable, you know? So, if you don't want to be here, at least stop wasting my bloody time.'

She rumbled on for what felt like an hour. I murdered her one hundred times over in my head. I like to force my fingers through her eyes and into her skull, though, that particular day I noticed a new Sellotape dispenser on her desk. (I notice the small things like that for some reason, it's just how my head is wired.) I grabbed her by the fat jaw, dragged her over to the desk, pushed her down, then wrapped tape over her face – mouth, nose, and all.

I flashed back, out of what I've now come to call a 'glitch', and left the office with the schedule in my hand without saying another word.

DIGITAL KILLED THE
ANALOGUE STAR

Digital projection was already taking over when I first started working at The Box. Back in the day they used film reels, but everything has changed – film reels are now a thing of the past. There was still one 35mm projector at The Box, set up in screen 10.

They only ever used it for special screenings of old

films, mainly horrors when they done all-night shows at Halloween. There's countless stories about screen 10 being haunted. I've never experienced any paranormal activity in there, although, it is a lot colder, so you never know.

Early on, the movies would arrive on small hard drives, and I'd load them onto the computer for each digital projector – unlocking the content with a code on a USB drive sent with the film. As digital seeped in, more and more like an incurable virus, I began loading the movies onto a central server – serving them up to each projector based on the screening schedule, along with pre-show adverts and trailers. Everything can be fully automated these days and it makes me sad as hell.

I was the only remaining full-time projectionist at The Box. Everyone else either left or got fired. They kept me on because I had the most experience and was competent at my job, even if my timekeeping wasn't the best. However, as The Troll had informed me earlier that day, I *was* replaceable.

The only thing that could replace me was digital technology, and I knew it was drawing ever closer to that day. What would I do then, become a popcorn pusher? Worse still, an usher? It was eating away at me, the guillotine closing in another inch with each passing hour.

Expendables 2 was released that day and they

were expecting the cinema to get busy, but it didn't. We put on three screenings, and I'd say about one hundred and thirty die-hard action fans turned up in total, which was a poor show. Time dragged by and I was agitated inside – the beetles scraping their way to the surface of my skin with no mercy.

STARMAN

I don't mingle well with the other employees at work. They all think I'm weird. They used to talk shit about me when I was upstairs in the projection rooms; making fun of my curly hair, thick glasses, and whatever else amused their small minds on any given day. I was dubbed 'Bowie' on my first day there because of my heterochromia – I have one blue eye and one brown eye like David Bowie. My surname, Moon, didn't help matters on that front. 'Starman' was another name people teased me with. The list goes on. There's a funny story behind the Starman nickname, but I'll get to that at some point further down the line.

GOAT AND OTHER TROUBLESOME THOUGHTS

I couldn't bear taking my breaks in the staff room back then. Instead, I sat in the locker room alone to get some peace and quiet. The locker room was musty, cramped, and unpleasant to look at. I soon grew accustomed to it. I sat in there eating my sandwiches, thinking too much about anything and everything. The horrible sense of dread was never far from my gut.

Is my house on fire? What if someone breaks into my car when I'm working? What if I crash on the way home? What will my nightmares be about tonight? Will it be the reoccurring nightmare again, the one I've had since I was a child, the one where the goat-devil is coming to get me, clambering up the wooden stairs in our old house?

I just never knew. I sat there eating my lunch and drinking my coffee during the day, scared about what was going to happen when I closed my eyes and went to sleep. I was a pathetic loser.

I had nobody to talk to about my demons. They built up inside of me like a fire, and I worried about what would happen when the blaze in my belly was finally too much for me to extinguish. *Where will it all come out?* This was one of the things pushing me over the edge, and I could feel myself getting closer and closer to jumping. I did almost kill myself, after all.

My mental health has always been fractured. Finding my mother dead at a young age didn't do too much to help matters. I can never remember feeling 'normal'. But that was just another blow. I didn't fit in well at school either, and I've always felt different inside. I find it hard to believe that other people think about the things I do, but they could be hiding behind masks. If the whole world is acting, everyone else is putting on a better show than I am.

I think people can sense it off me, the disease; their intuition hinting that something isn't right. It could be a sinister aura surrounding me, or even a putrid odour. My hands tremble and I sweat a lot, so that could also be the giveaway.

My doctor was like a robot, programmed to inform me it was natural to be feeling the way I was. We talked a lot about the massive shock of me finding my mother. He said the pain would always be there, that it would get easier as time went on. People are great believers in 'time heals everything'. I think it's a lot of old bullshit. If anything, the pain gets worse. It festers away like a fusty cider, fermenting in a hidden organic barrel in your colon.

My doctor was past his sell-by-date, maybe late sixties. His voice was deep, groggy, and reminded me of a grumpy dog's growl. He had this little wart on the tip of his nose – it's all I could focus on when I went to see him. I wanted to zap it with Medical Ice spray like they did to the wart on my finger when I was in primary school.

Nobody would partner up with me at my very first school dance because of that wart, not even the teachers. That was the first time I found out how traumatic being rejected could be.

My doctor tried me on a number of different medications until we found one that 'worked' – mirtazapine, with a side dose of diazepam to take the edge off. I'm not convinced the pills make any difference. I got to the stage that I couldn't get through to my doctor; it was like talking to a slab of concrete. I nodded, agreed, and told him everything he wanted to hear. I eat the pills but I'm not yet satisfied.

I went over the conversation I would have with the doctor – a million times in my head – when I was in bed the previous night. After the appointment my doctor put my prescription on repeat. I've not been back to see him since. I don't plan on ever going back. I was born like this. They can't put a bandage on my mind and fix me, no matter how prestigious the university degree. I am broken, rotten to the core. I am a walking, drinking, smoking, pill-popping virus.

Luna saved me. I'd be dead right now if it wasn't for her, burning in Hell. I'll definitely be taking up residence – at some point in the future – in the most diabolical circle for what I have done. My only goal now is to make the Devil tremble on my arrival.

Life will burn you to the bones, just remember to smile through the fire.

My shift felt like it was never going to end – I was close to hanging myself in hall 10 with a grease-stained apron – but it finally did. I hurried to the locker room, grabbed my bag, made my way down the corridor, and out into the foyer. Three vultures were standing around chatting at the top of the stairs about something uninteresting and not worth talking about in the first place.

They fell silent as I approached, huddled in closer together. I ignored them and skipped down the stairs to the main entrance. They starting sniggering and laughing as soon as I was gone. Christy was there – she was always the instigator. I wished them all a horrible death in my head as I escaped into the cool night air, free once again.

THE GLASWEGIAN AROMA

The first thing you notice in Glasgow, before the littered streets and graffiti, is the strong stench of urine, mixed with the previous night's vomit for good measure; on occasion the vomit is sprayed over shop-fronts like a street exhibition of bile-inspired Jackson Pollock paintings. Then you notice the polystyrene containers – half-filled with kebabs, chips, burgers, and salad – hugging the curb for dear life, assaulted the night before and left on the streets to die.

I have lived in Glasgow my whole life, so I am used to the city's many flaws. I like living in the city, it has character. I often go on long drives in the middle of the night when I can't sleep. I cruise the streets and suck it all up; the fluorescent lights in takeaway windows, drunk people stumbling out from the nightclubs, the music escaping from karaoke bars, and the sound of buskers performing original songs.

I'm an observer. I don't know if the talent for noticing the most intricate details about a person is a good thing or a bad thing, but it is a talent I possess, nonetheless.

I often hang about and listen for a while before

tipping the street performers. Some of them are fantastic and it puzzles me. *Why are such talented artists on the streets performing and not in a studio making records?* I tip them well.

The *X-factor*, and other garbage shows of a similar calibre, are ruining the music industry in much the same way money-hungry Hollywood suits are hell-bent on destroying the film industry with their terrible remakes, dreadful sequels, and the never ending shit-stream of unwatchable comic book movies.

SUPERMARKET BLUES

There's a 24 hour Asda next door to The Box. Before getting into my car and driving home, I went in to buy cigarettes and cat food for Luna. After spending the whole day in near darkness, my eyes were sensitive. They stung as I entered the supermarket and it took them a moment or two to adjust.

12:00AM is the perfect time to go shopping – it's empty, quiet, and you don't have to burrow your way through crowds of people that are more concerned with the chit-chatting than the task at hand. Those people don't go to Asda for shopping, it's more of a social extravaganza. I like to get in, avoid as much human interaction as possible, and get out without having a mental meltdown.

I grabbed a trolley on my way in. Like I said, 12:00AM is the perfect time, and it was dead. I could slide around the tiled floor at my own leisure. I made my way down to the pet food aisle, my feet clapping out a mellow melody as I strolled. I was the orchestra *and* the composer when I was alone in the supermarket.

I'd never had a cat before, or a pet for that matter; I could barely look after myself. The cat in the Felix advert is cute—well, I wouldn't go that far, but it was the only cat food brand I could think of at the time. I picked up a box of 24 pouches, chicken and liver in jelly.

I had a look at the cat toys. I was unaware of the vastness of the pet toy market. There was everything: balls, mice on string, an array of stuffed animals that squeaked when you squeezed them—there was even a house. I imagined Luna taking up residence in the house, it melted my heart. I picked up the box and placed it in the trolley.

I chucked in a few bowls and made my way to the collars. Most of them were pink. She'd look like Marie from *Aristocats* with the pink one, and that particular cat in the film annoyed the hell out of me. She was smug and the bow on her head was a step too far. The cuteness overload made her ugly.

After rummaging around I found an emerald green collar with a paw charm. I put it in the trolley, followed by a litter tray, then made my way to the kiosk to get cigarettes and check out.

There was a girl chatting to the man at the kiosk. My feet grew heavy; they were no longer gliding like butter, my orchestra had fallen flat, and the crowd had noticed my hands were composing like an alcohol-fuelled football fan. I was on a long, thick honey trail, leading me into the hive of social awkwardness, complete with a side of shaking hands and eye twitches. I continued on my way. *It's only one girl,* I tried to rationalize.

She had short hair. I think they call it a pixie cut, but don't quote me on that, I'm not a hairdresser. She wore a blue headscarf with paisley print. The closer I got to the kiosk, the more my mind was working on every single detail about the girl I didn't know. From the shoes she was wearing, to the colour she had painted her nails – mint-green.

I was over-analyzing everything; it's something my head does when I panic, or when I am in an uncomfortable situation. Most of the time I create these situations all by myself, but that's not the point.

I couldn't turn around and run away, for that would've made everything ten times worse, because they would see me trying to escape. When I finally built up the courage again I'd have to deal with the guy at the kiosk, and he'd be asking himself the whole time, *What the fuck is wrong with this guy?*

No, we couldn't have that, so I meandered, hoping she would be on her way by the time I reached the counter. That didn't happen. Her voice was now in ear's reach and I could make out parts of the conversation. The topic was employment. *Please don't be applying for a job at Asda, that's the road to Hell right there.*

She would become stuck in retail like Daniel Radcliffe was stuck as Harry. Old Harry boy had been typecast in the art of wizardry. This girl would be typecast in the art of ringing up balding creams, tampons, the dildo shampoo, Umberto Giannini, bathroom towels, toothpaste, spray tan in a can, avocados—fucking avocados. The lot. If you ever want to visit Hell before your time, get stuck in a retail position for ten years; the aisles and flickering fluorescent lights will guide you straight to Oblivion.

A little closer. I could smell her perfume, it was familiar to me. I couldn't put my finger on it at the time. There was a fruitiness to the perfume at the beginning, then the bitter vanilla undertones took over. And it went round and round in my nostrils on a continuous cycle – fruity, vanilla, fruity, vanilla. *I should've picked up some ice cream,* I thought, but it was too late. I was deep into the girl-at-the-counter situation and I couldn't run away. At this proximity I would look like even more of a weirdo than I already did, edging up behind her like a pervert.

I was standing right next to her. I couldn't see her face, so I checked her out from behind. She was wearing a vintage-yellow raincoat. The coat came down just above her ass. In that second, I remembered the first time I watched *Last Action Hero* on VHS. Ripper sported a similar raincoat in the film, though he also had a half-melted face and was a maniac. The girl in Asda pulled it off with class.

She was wearing a pair of skinny denims and I could tell she went to the gym more than once a week. *A girl has to work hard for an ass that good. Unless, of course, she was blessed by the angels of glut.* I later found out it was the latter.

Converse high-tops hugged her feet, and I noticed some blue and red paint splashed on the back of her left trainer. *An artist?* I always wanted to meet an artist, a real artist. I mean someone who still works for hours in a studio with watercolours, oils, acrylics. That kind of work is impressive to me because it's organic, raw, and the only foundation is a blank white canvas. Even the foundation is put together by the artist.

Another burst of fragrance shot into my nostrils. The guy had a piece of A4 paper in his left hand – I could make out 'CV' at the top. The paper was confirmation of a bad decision. *No,* said the voice inside my head. *Follow your dream of being an artist.* Which was rich coming from me, considering every story I'd written at that point had been rejected.

I shuffled in a little closer. *I wonder what her name is?* As the guy was placing the CV on the top of a pile under the counter, I tried to get a glimpse of her name. I caught only the first two letters – *R-O.*

'Thanks,' Ro said, walking away and out the automatic doors.

My heart dropped when she left. I didn't know what her face looked like and now I wanted to. Her voice was lyrical; husky, but not deep and haggard like that of Kathleen Turner.

THE POET AND THE ARTIST

There once was a poet and an artist. They fell in love at first sight. The Poet spent his days writing about life and the world around him. The Artist spent her days painting the same; it was romantic and everything was great—for a time.

The Poet fell into a deep depression. He became an alcoholic. One night, after a hardcore drinking session, he committed suicide.

The Artist was distraught, heartbroken, and confused. Why would he leave her to live alone in this godforsaken place?

The Artist vanished from existence, as though she had fallen off the face of the earth, never to be seen again.

There once was a poet and an artist. They fell in love at first sight and it destroyed them.

FACE/OFF

I slipped into a glitch. I was the Asda robot's husband. I pushed the shopping trolley and she held my free hand. We made a joke about who was going to cook dinner when we got home. We also made jokes about who was going to get to keep the pound coin from the trolley this time. I still couldn't make out her face – it was all smooth skin with no features, but I didn't mind. I held her hand anyway. I tried to kiss her and, when my lips made contact, her face started to melt and open up. Black holes appeared at the top, where her eyes should've been, and a huge dripping mouth gaped at the bottom of her face. She said something – it was deep and sounded like an EVP recording from that ridiculous show *Ghost Adventures*. You know, the ones that never seem to sound like what they tell you they sound like? I looked up at the sky, sunny and blue only moments before, as it turned a horrible, hazy, purple colour. Her hand broke free from mine. Even through the distorted, melted face, I could tell she was scared, terrified. She pointed up at the sky, gurgling more incoherent words, then lowered her hand to her head, mimicking a gun. There was a *bang*. Nothing happened—at first. The pound coin fell from the trolley a few moments later, rolled down the road, and into a drain. Tar-like tears oozed from the holes in her face. White smoke spewed from the dripping void that was her mouth. I w—

DAVE POIROT

'Hey, you okay? Excuse me, sir.'

I snapped back. The guy at the checkout was clicking his fingers at me.

'Feeling okay there? You're sweating buckets.'

I looked up. Ro was gone.

'Sorry,' I said.

My eyes focused in on the name badge, his name was Dave. *Why is everyone called Dave? Karen's homosexual Dave, Daves everywhere I go, and now this older gentleman stood before me—another fucking Dave.*

He looked a little like Hercule Poirot, although his moustache was an auburn colour. *How long has this one been caught in the supermarket trap?* He had been trapped long enough to have reached some kind of managerial status – he was dressed in plain clothes and not those horrible green shirts they make the other staff wear.

'I've not been feeling myself lately, you see?'

I wiped my head to show old Dave.

'You really don't look well.'

'I'll be fine, just one of those days, you know?'

'Try hammering twelve hour shifts in here six days a week.'

His moustache done the Mexican wave as he spoke. Old Dave scanned my stuff, packing it into the trolley for me.

'I know the feeling. I work at The Box, usually ten hour shifts, but sometimes they drag on and I don't get outta that place when I'm supposed to.'

'Ah, I like it in there, they play the oldies once in a while. Are they still doing that?'

'There's only one 35mm projector left. I give it a year and it'll be gone, maybe even six months.'

'That's a shame. Don't do it like they used to, eh?'

'I hear you. Wish they did.'

I tried a smile but my face felt like it was constipation time.

'Anything good showing at the minute?'

'Not really. Expendables 2, the Total Recall remake, both terrible. Are you a Cronenberg fan? Cosmopolis is playing, it's not bad.'

When is this small talk going to end? The guy was taking his time – I only had six or seven items in my trolley and it felt like I had known him since the day I was born.

'I do like a bit of Cronenberg, loved Scanners,'

'That's one of my favourites, especially the exploding heads.'

I forced one final smile and a nod. At least old Dave seemed to have half decent taste in cinema. Cronenberg—yet *another* Dave.

'Twenty Chesterfield Red as well, please.'

I smoked Chesterfield Red, solely because James Bond smoked them in *Goldfinger*. Old Dave passed over the carton of cigarettes.

'So, that comes to...£59.64.'

I handed him sixty quid, told him to put the change in the charity box, and left in a hurry. My feet were no longer dancing. The orchestra had long died.

I never knew it at the time, but the girl I hadn't met in my life before, the possible artist wearing the familiar perfume, the girl with the great ass – that girl was the person to change the course of my life forever.

HONEY, I'M HOME

My body shuddered as I pulled up in my driveway. The living room light was on, and the television – I could tell from the constant changing images and the blue glow shining through the blinds. I was freaked. Had someone robbed my house when I was at work? And if so, why did they leave the television? Stranger still, why had they put the television on in the first place – did they have a Netflix and chill session at my expense, binge watched a season of their favourite show before buggering off? I doubted it.

I opened the boot of my car, took out a hammer from my tool kit, then made my way inside. I opened the front door as quietly as I could; if there was someone in my house, I wanted to catch them unaware, and didn't want to give them the time to arm and compose themselves for a showdown. Although, if there *was* someone inside, the headlights from my car would have startled them already, giving them more than enough time to escape out the back door, unidentified.

I could hear the television as I walked down the hallway, it was blaring. The distinctive voice of James Gandolfini rang in my ears. Someone was, or had been, watching *The Sopranos*. My heart was fluttering, my stomach full of butterflies. As I approached the living room door, a bright image of the would-be intruder – hiding behind the door, waiting to stab me to death – surged through my rambling brain.

The anxiety was building up in my gut. I slid into the living room in one swift movement—there was nobody there. Luna, on the other hand, was sprawled out on the sofa. She looked up at me for a moment, lost interest, and placed her head on a cushion. I turned the volume down on the television and made my way into the kitchen.

The kitchen door was locked. I made my way upstairs and continued doing a sweep of my house; bedroom, en-suite bathroom, study. The anxiety eased off after a thorough investigation – there was no way someone had burgled the place. There was no sign of forced entry. I had locked all the windows before I left for work, (to ensure Luna stayed put) and they were all still locked. I was left scratching my head. *Maybe I left the television on when I was in a rush?*

I went back out to the car, placed the hammer in the boot, then carried in the shopping. After a long day of being lazy, Luna would have worked up an appetite. I wasn't hungry. I was more excited about putting the house together. Before that though, I checked on her wounds to make sure there was no infection setting in.

I made up a basin of warm water, rinsed the flannel I had used the night before, and went into the living room. I sat down next to Luna and lifted her onto my lap.

'How's the patient today?'

She knew what was coming. She resisted like an eel, put up a good fight, but finally gave in long enough for me to have a look at her. The cuts and grazes were healthy, no infection setting in. Still, I cleaned the wounds with the flannel cloth. Luna scurried towards the kitchen as I placed her down.

I put milk in her bowl and she was at it right away. I then opened a pouch of Felix and squeezed it into the other bowl. The stuff smelled disgusting, although, Luna would beg to differ. She went between bowls, spoiled for choice.

'I've got a surprise for you.'

The cat house didn't take long to build. There was a ground floor and an upper level. On the roof, a long scratching post acted as a chimney, and a plump duck on a string dangled out the top. I was surprised at how tall it was, standing about three and a half foot.

'Luna, come and see what I've got for you.'

Her little paws skipped over the wooden floor. She poked her fuzzy face into the living room and had a peek, then took a short dash and leaped onto the roof, torturing the duck with all four paws.

I poured myself a tall glass of Scotch – this time, instead of adding a deadly mix of crushed up pills, I added four ice cubes. The day had been long and I was dead, but I like having a drink after work to take the edge off.

My eyes were heavy and my brain was full. *Who was that girl? What was that perfume? I should've went back for ice cream.*

I sat on the sofa and opened Netflix. Luna bounced up onto my lap and snuggled in. I browsed for a minute before coming across *Scanners* – it must have been fate. I clicked *Play*.

I lit a cigarette and the smoke danced up my face. Savouring the sweet taste of poison, I settled back on the sofa and put my feet up on the coffee table. For a moment, for the very first time in years, I didn't feel lonely.

THURSDAY WITH KAREN

The delivery comes in on a Thursday and I get to help unload it with Karen. She bends down a lot as she picks up the smaller boxes; I'd be lying if I said I didn't notice. You would have to be blind to miss a sight like that. I took care of the heavier boxes, which I didn't mind.

Everyone else was busy pushing popcorn and tooth-rot, cleaning, gossiping, and indulging in other mindless non-work related activities. At 14:16PM on a Thursday, all the films were set up and running, giving me time to help Karen for a couple of hours. We got through the delivery in an hour, team work and all that.

Karen was the only person I had real conversations with at work, more than just the false chit-chat that I had to put up with when I was forced to talk to anyone else at The Box. She'd ask me about my love life and if I had any girls on the go. The answer was always a straight-up no.

'You been up to anything exciting recently?'

She asked, picking up a box of Skittles.

'Not much to be honest, I'm always in here.'

'Tell me about it, Dave hates the hours I do in here. He doesn't realise we have bills to pay, thinks everything is a joke.'

Dave was an award-winning barber, but he busted his back in a road accident and was off on the sick, moping around at home, playing his guitar. He even updated his Facebook page to inform the world he was now a 'singer-songwriter'.

'That sucks. How's the old back? Any better?'

'Don't even get me started. I think he's at it. He

sits at home all day playing his guitar, trying to write songs. Says he's going on the X-Factor next year.' She rolled her eyes.

'Really? You never know.'

'Trust me, the man doesn't have a musical bone in his body. Yeah, he can strum a few chords on his guitar, but he's hardly the next John Lennon. Simon Cowell would eat him alive if he went on the X-Factor. I'd be mortified.'

'That bad?'

'That bad.' Karen replied, then changed the subject. 'You got a girlfriend yet?'

'Nah, too much hassle.'

I'd only ever been in one real relationship before, with a girl called Kat, and it crashed and burned after a year. She said I was mental, erratic, and hard work. The thing I found hysterical is the fact she was a registered mental health nurse. Kat left one Christmas without telling me. I never heard from her again. I checked her Facebook the other week and she's going out with some guy called Spencer, fucking Spencer. He looks like a heroin addict. Anyway, that's another story with little significance to this one.

'C'mon, a good looking guy like you could have his pick of the crop.'

I could feel my cheeks going red. Karen looked up at me and winked. *God, don't do that when you're bending over.* Her ass was popping in all the right places.

'I'm glad you think so.'

'Curly hair and glasses are in at the minute. Maybe just tame the mane once in a while.'

'*Maybe* I'll take your advice.'

I checked my watch. I had to get back soon.

'Hey, my niece has an interview in here today, she's cute. And most importantly, she's single.'

'Mixing work with relationships is a disaster waiting to happen.'

'Nonsense. She's kinda geeky like you...I don't mean that in a bad way. You'd like her.'

My interest was piqued, if only for a second. *Wouldn't it be wonderful to be with someone who gets me? To share the nights chatting about the universe, our favourite movies, books, and actors?* I was kidding myself.

'What's her name?'

'Ah, see, you are interested. It's Robyn.'

R-O. Robyn? Stranger things have happened.

'Was just wondering.'

'She's a sweet girl. Erin is doing her interview though, so I'm not holding my breath. Hope she gets the job though.'

'Me too.'

We laughed. I checked my watch again.

'Anyway, I'll have to get back now, that okay?'

'Yeah, on you go. Just about finished anyway.'

'Cool, see you in a bit.'

'Don't work too hard.'

Karen smiled and got back to lifting boxes.

DO YOU EVER FEEL LIKE SOMEONE'S WATCHING YOU?

I arrived home at 01.00AM. The television was on. I checked and double checked that morning, so there is no way I left it on. Like before, I grabbed the hammer from the boot of the car. As I was about to make my way inside, I stopped dead.

Have you ever had the feeling someone's watching you? As though you are, for a change, the one being observed? It makes my skin dance all over with goosebumps. When I get that sensation I drift from my own body and, from afar, I scrutinize my second self. It's like there's two of me in existence, sharing the exact same moment in time.

There is a theory if you were to time travel, and confronted another version of yourself during said time travel, the world would implode. One mistake from a single man or woman could destroy the world as we know it—hypothetically.

Had I time travelled from the future? That

theory was unlikely, but the dreamlike sensation stayed with me for days after. I couldn't explain it. Most of my deepest fears are irrational and misunderstood – false evidence appearing real.

I hovered in the doorway for a second, gazing into the early morning silence, before making my way inside. I walked down the hallway and into the living room. Luna was on the sofa. I was about to do a sweep of the house when I noticed the television remote poking out from under her. Now it made sense. The television *must* have been on standby, and she *must* of hit the power button. Mystery solved...

I stroked Luna for a few minutes, having a good look at her injures – they were healing well. She'd regained some energy and was more playful. I fed her and emptied the litter tray, poured myself a glass of Scotch, and sat down in front of the television with my feet on the coffee table.

This had always been my daily routine when I got home from work – the only change was when I sat down on the sofa and put my feet up, Luna now pounced onto my lap and snuggled in. My sitting down was her cue. It turns out cats are better company than I imagined they would be.

FUR COATS AND HARD DRUGS

'What shall we watch tonight...Goodfellas? A fine choice.' Luna looked at me like I was stupid.

Goodfellas is one of those films that makes being a gangster look cool. However, as the film gets going, the body count gets higher. Everyone is out of their fucking minds with paranoia and people are getting whacked left, right, and center.

The glamour soon fades and you decide you no longer want to be a gangster. You would still like to have the beautiful girls, the fast cars, fur coats, and the continuous flow of hard drugs. You can't have it all though. Is a fur coat and unlimited grams of cocaine really worth it? I'm going to say no, but at least you'd go out like a total badass—or like a whimpering dog, when it really came down to it.

You've got to love the scene in *Goodfellas* when Joe Pesci borrows his mother's kitchen knife – she doesn't bat an eyelid when he asks to borrow it – to stab a guy to death in the back of a motor. The sick side of me cherishes that moment, and I often imagine that I'm right there, the one doing the plugging. If I think about it hard enough I can feel the knife in my hand, cutting flesh. I can even smell the blood.

NOCTURNAL HELL

The nightmares invaded my sleep about a month after my mum committed suicide. The doctor said it was post traumatic stress and would fade in time. However, the intensity has increased over the years. There is one nightmare in particular that terrifies me – it's a reoccurring dream I have most nights. Sometimes it's vague and hazy, other times it's vivid, tack-sharp, and real. On that particular night it was the latter.

My mum has just tucked me up in bed and kissed me good night. We always say the prayer together: *This night as I lay down to sleep, to God I give my soul to keep, if I should die before I wake, I pray the Lord my soul to take.* I'm not a religious person, far from it, but that prayer was always comforting to me as a child.

She makes her way back down stairs. I can hear the dull rumble of the television escaping from the living room. I find it soothing. I fall asleep. Some time passes, although, it's like I'm awake, even when my eyes are closed.

The room is dark when I shoot up from my bed, the air is thick, and I'm sweating profusely. I still don't realise I'm dreaming. I'm petrified and I can sense something in the room with me. A sinister presence. I sit there frozen for a minute—and then I hear it.

A frantic clambering on the wooden stairs in the hallway – like a horse trying to escape from a trailer – and it's getting closer, louder with each passing second. It struggles to reach the top, aggression in every frenzied step, doing whatever it takes to get there.

Why is it trying to get to the top landing with so much determination? The only thing up here is— and that's when the fear becomes more real, because I know the main purpose for the creature tackling the stairs is to get to *me*.

My heart drops like a stone. I spin round in my bed in a delayed, sluggish motion, and drift to my feet. I fumble around in the top drawer of my bedside cabinet, pulling out a Power Rangers torch – a desired birthday present of that year. I click it on and the Black Ranger illuminates the room as I search for a weapon to protect myself.

On the wall, directly above my bed, I notice the fawn foot hunting knife my dad recently passed down to me. The creature is getting closer. I can hear his heavy grunting; he struggles for air as though he's suffocating, and it sounds like a mucus-infested, rattling growl. I grab the hunting knife from the wall and pull it from the sheath.

I am brave with the knife in my hand, even though I'm trembling. I click the torch off, cloaking myself in darkness. My aim is to make my way out onto the hallway, have a look over the railing at the top of the stairs, and discover the creature trying so desperately to get to me.

I venture out of the safety of my bedroom and onto the landing, tiptoeing into the unknown terror of the night. Most kids would duck under the covers and close their eyes – I wasn't like other children. I had a curious lust for adventure and, if I was ever scared, I had to discover the source of fear.

Curiosity killed the cat.

I approach the railing with caution. There's a putrid smell in the air and the sound of the clambering vibrates in my ears.

I can hear him gulping the air—*if I can smell him, hear him breathing, can he also smell me?* A shock jolts through my stiff body. I prepare to look over the railing...everything goes silent. I lean over and look down the stairwell—nothing. I pull up my Power Rangers torch and point it towards the source of fear, *click-click.*

And there he is, looking up at me, a metre from my face. He howls and shrieks. I want to run away but my feet are nailed to the floor. I am stuck looking at the creature, dead in his soulless eyes.

He is half man and half—something else. A deformed goat. His gloss-black hooves hammer the stairs. The torso is muscular, human. His face is vile; worse than any comic book villain I have ever encountered.

The horns are crooked, a mucky blood-red colour, all twisted and chipped upon his demon head. The thing standing in front of me is a battle-hardened monster, tormenting children his lifelong career. Saliva drips from his open mouth as he howls, the teeth overlapping like that of a shark's many layers. They are yellow and rotten – the root of the rancid breath he heaves. I gag and throw up.

Can he see my thoughts, the cogs turning in my mind? I struggle to escape his gaze. He has some kind of hypnotic hold over me, but I manage. I bolt to my room, scurry under my covers, and hide like a normal child.

I click the torch off and listen, clutching the hunting knife with both hands, waiting on the inevitable arrival of the monster. *Is he the Devil? Is he here to collect my soul?*

He is coming. Faster now. Closer now. He is almost here. I suck in the air, hold it, and close my eyes. *Maybe he won't find me if I stay here like this.* And then I wish I hid *under* the bed. *Surely it would be harder for him to get me under there?* There is no time to move.

He kicks his hooves back and forth like a raging bull on the landing floor, though he doesn't charge. He composes himself and prepares, taking control of the atmosphere, and makes his way to my room.

The bedroom door creaks as he enters, his claws rattling on the doorknob. He's coming right for me. I can smell his foul breath, can feel the warmth of it through my duvet—I jump from my covers, eyes closed, swiping the knife in random slashing motions in every direction, cutting the creature to shreds.

The light comes to life, stealing the darkness. Standing there bleeding from the gut, the throat, the eyes, bleeding from everywhere, is my mother. She falls to the ground, clutching her throat on the way down, eyes rolling in the back of her head.

On the bang from her fall, I spring up in my bed, startled, disorientated, and sweating like a pig.

I'm drained when I wake from the nightmare, even more tired than I was before I went to bed in the first place; it's a savage dream that rips my soul apart. Everything comes crashing back into my mind, destroying my thoughts. The image of my mother lying dead on the floor burns my retinas. The guilt of killing her over and over again consumes me. I question if it's my fault she's no longer in the land of the living.

A SOLDIER OF MISFORTUNE

My mood was shot to shit in the morning. *Here comes the self-loathing.* Luna was sleeping at the foot of my bed, but I felt no comfort in her being there. I was back at base camp with a mountain in front of me, taunting me, waiting to be climbed once again. What's the point of being on top? Being on top means you have much farther to fall. Wouldn't it be better to stay at the bottom and wallow in all the shit? Sure, that's not a very happy place to be, but at least you know it can't get any worse, no sudden curve-balls. A fucking veteran in the art of fighting depression. No surprises, no frilly knickers, just sadness and dismay. A soldier of misfortune, trapped in the claustrophobic trenches with the peasants; the children forced to fight another battle that they are too young to comprehend. Dehydrated, starving, terrified, and for what reason? The outcome is always the same. Death and destruction. And if you are unlucky enough to survive, what then? Well then, may God help your weeping soul.

I climbed out of bed and stretched – my back was aching. I had slept in an awkward position, curled up like a restless foetus. I got in the shower to wash and ended up just standing there, my mind racing, the negative images polluting my eyes. There was no point in trying to stop them, it's better to let the negativity run its course. Battling the invasion – or focusing on a single image – brings on a migraine. The headaches are brutal and make me physically sick. Migraines are another thing in my life that I wish I could rid myself of.

I'm cursed, I swear to God, and I probably was from the day of conception. I must have committed an atrocious act in another life to be handed such a shitty card. I'm nothing but a ghost, trapped in this pathetic meat puppet, eroding my way to the casket.

The only reason I believe in a god is the fact that I believe in the possibility of a devil. Now, don't let the imagery of what I've just said get in the way. I don't mean some guy in the clouds that made the world in seven days. I'm not talking about angels and temptation. What I *am* talking about is a higher power. Something beyond man, something stranger than fiction. Something that even the greatest minds in our lifetime struggled to understand. Believing in a god that claps his hands and fixes everything is ridiculous. Nothing but a coping mechanism. For if we have nothing to believe in, then we are truly lost.

My mother was a religious person, and still she died by her own hand – a cardinal sin. What pushed her do that? If she was a child of God, wouldn't he have extended his huge, National Lottery-like hand and saved her? My mother is burning in eternal damnation. It doesn't make any sense to me.

I envy the people who can put one hundred percent faith into the Bible, a book that has been disproved a thousand times over. I guess that's where the 'faith' part comes in. When it comes down to it, we are all fucking lost, navigating our way through this mysterious land.

No wonder people get depressed and lonely. When we open our eyes and realise we have no real business existing here on this planet, what are we to do? Some people get so caught up in trying to figure out the meaning of life, myself included. We were put here with no map and no road signs to guide us.

We grow, we eat, we shit. If we are lucky enough to be born in a developed country, we go out, we squander our lives, we fuck, we sin, we drink ourselves half to death. We do drugs, listen to heavy metal, and denounce the world. We cause pain by telling lies and by performing manipulative actions. We cheat. We contract several sexually transmitted diseases because we can't keep our pants up and crave to be loved. We spread said diseases, we kill defenceless animals for profit, we step over the guy in front of us to advance ourselves a little more. We are greedy, we rape, we pillage, we *murder,* destroy, and at the end of it all we ask for forgiveness, just in case some guy with a white beard and a son called Jesus – who happens to be the same guy – died for our sins. He may well hear our prayers, accept our confessions of guilt, and open the gates to the clouds of purity. What a crock of old shit. I am more likely to believe that we are bastard children of ancient aliens, left behind to rot in our own filth

I DIDN'T HAVE
THAT FRIDAY FEELING

I couldn't be bothered getting ready for work, it was a constant struggle. Working on a Friday isn't all that bad, a lot busier, but not bad. I sometimes prefer working when it's heaving because it keeps my mind occupied, to a certain point, and the day flashes by.

Luna was awake when I got out of the shower and watched me getting dressed. She followed behind as I made my way down the stairs. A cold shiver tickled my spine as I got to the bottom. I made my way into the kitchen and fixed some food and milk for Luna. She was used to this routine now – her tail always saluted the sky when she was hungry.

I made a bacon and cheese toastie and sat down

at the kitchen table. There was a gurgling in my gut, and the sound of myself eating was getting on my nerves. Everything was so lonely and still. The sound of my own chewing echoed, making my ears bleed. I took one more shattering bite before putting most of the toastie in the bin. I'm sure I don't suffer from misophonia. Then again, my brain feels like it's all mushed, so it's a possibility.

I pulled on my parka jacket as it was raining outside, grabbed my car keys, and left.

I didn't even say goodbye to Luna that morning. I felt like a Zombie. *Welcome to the land of the fucking undead. I want to eat your brains and drink your blood.* The bitter air attacked my face and the light pierced my eyes.

Angus was standing at the top of the stairs when I arrived at The Box.

'Ah, Freddy. Just the man.'

He had a forced expression on his face.

'What's up?'

'C'mon into the office and I'll get you a cuppa, I've got something I need to talk to you about.'

'Cool.'

I followed him to the office.

Erin was sitting at the desk with a smug look on her face. I noticed she had finally washed her hair, although it didn't do all that much for her – she still looked like a fat troll. I didn't say hello, I just sat down across from her and stared at the carpet. The kettle boiled in the background, followed by the stirring of cups. A few moments later, Angus appeared with the coffee. He took his seat. I knew then that something was going down, and I'd be lying if I said I wasn't worried. My stomach was churning.

'So, you've been with us for quite a while now, and you're a valuable member of the team.' Angus started.

'But?' I said.

'Well, this is a tough one for me. You see—'

Erin butted in with her greasy chops and took the limelight.

'We're going full digital and it's happening over the weekend, so we won't be needing you.'

A rogue basketball bounced into my throat.

'You're firing me?'

Angus reasserted himself and managed to regain control of the conversation.

'Now, wait a minute, we're storming ahead of ourselves. We don't want to get rid of you, that's the thing.'

'But she just said there wasn't going to be a job for me here after the weekend.'

'The thing is, we will no longer be needing you in your *current* position, but there are other positions available. We are taking on two new members of staff to join the team. I thought it would be only fair to offer you one of the positions.'

Is this fuck asking me if I want to join the others, pushing popcorn?

Erin was holding back a gut full of laughter, revelling in my misfortune, the sick bitch. I forced my fingers through her glasses, crushing the broken shards into her eyes. I picked up the mug of coffee sitting in front of me and poured it over her head, then grabbed a set of scissors from the desk and slit her throat. The blood squirted out all over the place in a fountain display of dark reds and I could taste the stench of her in my mouth.

'What would that entail? Selling popcorn with a stupid hat on my head?'

'Look, I'm sorry you feel that way, it's not that bad. And you know we need to wear the hats for hygiene reasons.'

I was speechless. I knew when I woke up it was going to be a crappy day, but I definitely wasn't expecting to be fired.

'We could always set you up at the ticket booth, would you prefer that? No hat. You'd rotate between selling tickets, collecting tickets from customers, and screen checks?'

I suppose it was a compromise. Not a very good one, but it was a compromise nonetheless. At least

I'd get to act like Ethan Hunt when I was doing the screen checks with the night vision goggles – I'd always wanted to try them.

'I guess it's better than working up at the popcorn counter. When would I be starting, today?'

'Well, I was going to say you could come in and start fresh on Monday, how about that?'

I couldn't turn it down, I needed my job. Angus had me by the balls and Erin was twisting them into submission. She wanted me to quit. If there was no other reason to stay, staying to piss her off would have to do.

'Okay, that's fine.' I swallowed what was left of my pride.

'I'm sorry, I really am. I know how much you love your job, but we need to move with the times. We're lagging behind all the other cinemas in Britain. Glad you're staying with us though, wouldn't be the same without you.'

I go unnoticed every day, even though I'm the one who cares about the motion pictures, keeping them rolling and all.

'Look, take today off. Come in on Monday and we'll take it from there, how does that sound?'

'Sure. I know this isn't your fault.'

I glared at Erin. The disgust in my eyes must have been strong, she didn't know where to look.

'No hard feelings?' Angus said.

'No hard feelings, man.'

I shook his hand. He rustled around in a drawer and handed me a shirt wrapped in plastic.

'A medium should do you, yeah?'

It pained me to take the shirt.

'That should fit fine. One other thing, what about screen 10? Are we at least keeping that for the special screenings? Surely there's still some life in that yet?'

'Sadly not.' He concluded.

My heart sank a little more, and I could feel it escaping from the hole in my sock. *What kind of fucking witch hunt is this?* I stood up and left without saying another word.

My head was spinning and I wanted to spew in the middle of the foyer – everyone watching me choking my guts up would have been horrendous. I was becoming more paranoid with each passing day. *They* were watching me. In reality that wasn't the case, but it was in my head. I wasn't that much of an exciting person to study.

I made my way outside. I was glad to feel the cool breeze on my face. The sweat that had accumulated on my brow was blasted on impact. I took deep breaths – in through my nose and out through my mouth – to calm myself down and, after a while, it worked. My heart rate slowed back to normal, although I still felt light-headed, as if I wasn't there; halfway between dreaming and being awake.

I had experienced this kind of thing before, another symptom of anxiety. Everything was a symptom of anxiety, according to my doctor. If I was ever seriously ill they would miss it. I could be dying of cancer and they'd still say it was anxiety. What a joke.

What am I going to do now? I thought, standing there against the wall. I pulled out a cigarette from my carton and slapped it between my lips. My job was perfect; it kept me sane, I was interested in what I was doing for a living, and I didn't have to work too closely with anyone. I got the schedule in the morning, followed it, and left. Simple.

They had given me another position – which would mean less money at the end of the month – but that's not what was bothering me. The thing bothering me the most was the fact that I would need to face the public. Serving tickets and smiling every day was going to be a big task. I wasn't sure if I would be able to hack it. I had never worked face-to-face with the public before. I was always the ghost in the background, that's the way I liked it.

My stomach churned over and over, getting worse the more I thought about it. I wanted to curl up right there and let the ground swallow me up whole, I really did.

I composed myself after a while and made my way over to my car. I climbed in, put the keys in the ignition, and started her up. I had nowhere to be, nothing to do for the whole weekend, and now this— another full day of overthinking. There's nothing to do when you're alone and socially awkward. *Go home and hammer yourself into a state of alcohol-fuelled disability.* There was nothing else for it.

FOOTBALL IS NOT MY FORTE

Who would I be working with at the ticket desk?

Christy worked down at the ticket booth with another girl called Laura. I didn't know much about Laura, she kept herself to herself, and I can't remember having a single conversation with her. Christy, on the other hand, hated me. And I mean she despised me. The feeling was more than mutual.

Christy was a mammoth. She was too tall, overweight, and had a five o'clock shadow on her top lip. *She should think about getting that thing waxed off, it's hideous.*

I was once forced to play at a charity football event – something I had no interest in being a part of. Old Angus had convinced me it would be fun. He also cracked the whip and reminded me it was part of my job. There was no way out of the situation, so I bit my tongue and got on with it.

The tournament was between all The Box staff from every region in Britain, and was to be a full day event. I wasn't looking forward to it.

If there is one thing I hate in this world, it's football. I hate football with a passion. I've never been able to understand the fascination with kicking around a bag of air. I feel quite similar towards golf. At least with golf you get to crack the shit out of something with a metal stick – a wonderful stress reliever – giving the sport a greater purpose. *Is that why so many old married guys are into playing golf?* I've also noticed that golf players live longer – that's not a statistic from a medical journal or anything, it's just my own observation.

They needed one more player to complete our team, and the lucky player was yours truly. Christy was the team captain, even though she'd never jogged more than a step or two in her life. Maybe a few more when she was running to the front door to collect a Chinese takeaway, no doubt. Christy being the team captain is where we clashed, setting a chain of downward spiralling events into motion.

The first thing that made me angry was the fact everyone else had brand new football kits. I didn't have so much as a pair of shorts, so she gave me an old football strip that a previous employee had used a couple of years earlier. A great start to making me feel like part of the team. The thing was a mile too big and drooped around my waist like a dress. I could roll the sleeves up, tuck the shirt into my shorts, but there wasn't much I could do about the yellow stains under the armpits. (I took the shirt home and boil washed it in an attempt to eradicate the piss-coloured blotches. They didn't budge.)

Christy didn't put me on the field at the event – she kept me as a substitute for the whole day. *What is the point of me even being here?* I thought. The weather was terrible. I spent most of the day standing at the sideline in the lashing rain. She walked over to me at one point to rub it in.

'Cheer up, Bowie, you look like you're on another planet there.'

I didn't acknowledge her and kept my eyes on the flooded grass. There was a worm slithering over a slug. They moved in slow motion together – it calmed my mind and focused my train of thought. So many people miss the little things in life. Twenty-six years of living and I had never come across a worm slithering over a slug. I was witnessing a once-in-a-lifetime event and Christy was shitting all over it. She'd probably block out a solar eclipse to spite me.

Christy deliberately kept me from participating. And I bet they all had a right good laugh about it. I had never done anything to upset her in the past, so

I couldn't understand why she was treating me like I was an idiot. I cracked her on the back of the head with a hammer, but she didn't seem to mind. She walked away singing, 'Starman...'

And that's where the nickname came from.

I was fuming. I chewed on my lips and murdered her. I had already murdered her a few times throughout the day, but the hammer felt the best – her thick skull crunching like an Easter egg. Happy fucking Holidays.

I prayed to every god – even the ones I don't believe in – that something terrible would happen to her. The violent thoughts helped to keep me calm.

I was a huge David Bowie fan when I was younger, and I bet he didn't fit in at school either. I should have taken it as a compliment. Either way, Christy had pissed me off, so I tried to focus my anger on something else.

I revisited the worm and the slug, but then I remembered a billboard I noticed on the way there. The billboard claimed: '*We make an average of thirty-five thousand choices in a single day – Make them count.*'

The cogs in my head powered on as I calculated how many choices I had made in my pathetic life— an average of 332,150,000 is what I got. *How many choices do I have left? How many choices have I wasted on self-loathing and empty, one-sided love?*

GOD SAVE THE SWEET MERLOT

There was an award ceremony at the end of the day. The Glasgow region came last, which was the only thing that made me smile over the duration of the trip. The embarrassment was strong and all the other teams teased our players. I got some twisted pleasure from it all.

I wanted the whole thing to be over – it dragged on forever and I wanted to die. Food and drinks followed the ceremony, extending our stay even longer.

There was a fierce tension between the team. They growled at me from every direction. They, the great ones, the clique of doom, after all, were the one's who lost the game. They should think twice about casting a couch potato as the team captain next time.

It could have been my lack of interest in the game that offended them, or my smirking at the awards ceremony when they announced that our team was last. There's something wrong with you if you cry over a plastic medal, and that's saying a lot coming from me. Christy had a face like thunder. Her cheeks were red and I could tell she was going to explode at some point.

Twelve of us occupied the same table and, out of all those people, Christy was situated directly across from me. A few of the staff made small talk as we waited on our food. Everyone ate in near silence when the food arrived. I was taking a bite out of my chicken burger when I happened to look up, and there she was, staring right back at me; an ogre, a parasite, a fucking cancer, eating away my precious dead soul with a glaring expression on her bloated face.

'What you looking at, freak?' Christy said.

The insults kept coming, thick and fast. *You're a weirdo, nobody even likes you, you're so creepy*—to name a few. On the inside I was boiling over, but I didn't open my mouth, which made her even more angry. Angus butted in after a while.

'That's totally uncalled for.'

He was never angry – a laid back guy – though I'm glad someone said something to take the heat away from me for a second. Everyone else sat in silence, eyes rolling around the room like pool balls on a dodgy table – always moving, never quite reaching a target.

As it later turned out, Christy was the girl from the rumour. The rumour involving Angus sleeping with an eighteen year old member of staff, forcing her to have an abortion, and then paying her £200 smackers to keep the whole thing on the down low. I enjoyed the plot twist.

I'm glad I didn't know that at the time, because I would have blurted it out all over the place, most likely losing my job in the process of slut shaming Christy. Looking back I can see that Angus was the only one who could keep Christy under control. He had some kind of hold over her, and I think she held a sick and twisted love for the man.

'I've so had it with him. He's such a fucking loser, makes my skin crawl.'

Christy continued. I couldn't hold my tongue any longer.

'I'm not exactly your biggest fan either, you make me physically sick. I think it's the moustache. Why don't you get that thing waxed off or something? I feel more ill every time I I look at it, and I've been stuck looking at it all day long.' I ranted.

Everyone jumped on-board after I defended myself. They all sided with Christy, of course. I wasn't surprised.

Christy stood up – quicker than I had ever witnessed her moving before – and stormed towards me, shouting absurdities and pointing her diva sausage fingers like a confused drag queen. I was expecting a slap on the jaw. I could've moved, although I stayed in my seat as a final act of defiance. The storm was coming and I was ready to ride it out.

Everything moved in Matrix-style motion. I was Neo. I tried to duck my head out the way—I wasn't The One. There was a surge of liquid coming straight for me and all I could do was take it like a little bitch. The red wine hit me square in the face, splashed up my nose, and made me cough. Twenty-four shock-filled eyes plagued me. A few sniggers followed the commotion, one belch of laughter in the distance. *Bastards.*

I sat there for a few seconds before springing to my feet. I wanted to ram a pint glass into her face. I also didn't like the idea of going to prison. Instead, I used the first thing that came to my hand—a chicken burger loaded with cheese, lettuce, plenty of mayonnaise, and hot sauce. I smashed it into her face with my fist.

'Eat that you fat fuck.'

I guess you could say that was the turning point for me. A glimmer of the beast had escaped. There was something evil inside of me, something eating away at my being. Gnawing. Taunting. A primal thirst for blood and destruction by my own hands. I had been suppressing the anger for too long. I was born with these desires and fantasies implanted in my mind and it felt good to lash out for real.

I wanted to physically murder a girl for wasting a glass of red wine on my face. I think I would have indulged in said fancy if it wasn't for the many rubberneckers surrounding us, I really do. I ripped her intestines out with a dessert fork – abdominal vandalism – and savoured the stench of her sweet blood as it warmed my face. I prayed it wasn't Merlot. God save the sweet Merlot.

CHEAP WHISKEY AND CIGARETTES

I arrived home with all the necessary supplies a depressed man would need to drown his sorrows for a weekend: four litres of Highland Earl whiskey, twenty-four bottles of Midnight Sun ruby porter, eighty Chesterfields, and an exhausted heart. At this rate I'd be a full-blown alcoholic by the end of the year. Perhaps I already was. I was on the road to self-destruction that weekend, for sure. And the weekend did not disappoint.

The first thing I did when I got home was pour a glass of whiskey and slammed it back, neat. I wanted to do the job right. I then opened a bottle of beer and started on that as I put out some food and milk for Luna. She kind of looked at me as though she knew I had received some bad news when I was out. They say cats and dogs can sense these things, which I'm inclined to believe.

After feeding Luna, I grabbed the bottle of whiskey, opened another bottle of beer, and made my way into the living room. I often enjoyed the silence, but not on that day. The sound of silence was making me feel empty and lonely as hell, so I turned on the television.

I watched *Twin Peaks* from the beginning – I was a huge fan and I had already watched the full show. I didn't have to burn too much brain power to follow the story. The main thing was to fill the place with some kind of noise. Anything would do, anything was better than the deafening silence.

I needed to switch my mind off, stop it from spinning into overdrive mode. I convince myself that alcohol helps to calm my mind, and maybe it does for a short while. The morning after I've been drinking heavily, the anxiety is worse than ever. I sweat like a maniac, I spew, I shit a lot, and I think about the most bizarre things – my head chugging along like a rusty old Ferris wheel.

I don't know why I continue to drink when it makes me feel so edgy the following day, it makes no sense. When I'm down, and my brain is fused, there isn't much that *does* make sense.

Luna sat on my lap, a novice enjoying *Twin Peaks* for the first time, and I threw back the bruskies like a man possessed. I was gone by

7:00PM. I hadn't eaten anything for most of the day, which helped me on my way to getting totally hammered. I grew agitated after a while. I needed to get up and move around, so I did. I was soon pacing around on the living room floor like a caged animal at the zoo.

The more drunk I got, the more depressed I became. The isolation wasn't helping matters. *I have to get out more,* I thought. *Karen said that finding a girlfriend would do me good. Would it?* I was warming to the idea.

My pacing was becoming more vigorous. I kept moving. Up and down, up and down. The sound of my shuffling feet on the floor grated my nerves paper thin. *If I'm annoying myself this much, how annoying am I to other people?*

Finding a girlfriend is a hard task in most situations. Finding a girlfriend when I was riddled with depression, self-loathing, and trapped inside my own bubble was going to be even more difficult. And where would I even meet this fantasy girl that I was now becoming more fond of in my head?

One hour, and a huge amount of overthinking later, I decided that finding a girlfriend would be in my best interest. It would help me come out of my shell – train me in the art of wearing my mask like the other 'normal' people in this deceptive society.

I sat back down on the sofa, took a slug of

whiskey from the bottle. *Twin Peaks* was still playing in the background and I had long lost interest. I kept it running to block out the silence, even though I could hardly focus on the television screen. My eyes were blurry and I was seeing double – two Luna's on my lap, two Dale Coopers excitedly sipping on two cups of fresh coffee with two doughnuts in each hand.

Whiskey, cigarettes, beers, pills. That is how the night went on before I slouched down on the sofa in silence, a good silence. My eyes were as heavy as kettle bells. When I closed them over I couldn't open them again. Everything went black as I slipped away into the empty void of drunken darkness.

MIRTAZAPINE DREAMS

My heart bounced into action. I had been stabbed in the chest with a needle full of adrenaline. I shot up and gasped for air like Mia Wallace in *Pulp Fiction*. Fear was creeping into my bones. *What disturbed me?* I was deep in a drunken slumber. I may have been dreaming, but I wasn't convinced. There was a voice. I heard it only once, a single word in an urgent tone.

The living room was in dead. I was blind, besides the red led light on the television, which had went into standby mode as there had been no action in so long. I was soaking wet and, for a brief moment, I thought I had pissed my pants. There was an unfamiliar odour lingering in the stale air. The atmosphere had changed. The silence was soon disturbed again by a fierce *hiss*.

I darted to my feet and hurried over to the light switch on the wall. My eyes took a moment to focus as the living room light beamed overhead. Luna came running in to meet me from the hallway. Her hackles were up and she was spooked.

She circled in and out of my legs. I picked her up, held her close to my chest, and made my way into the kitchen. I fumbled for the light switch. The security of a light goes a long way – the fear of the unknown is what makes the darkness so daunting. It's the same when you're bobbing in the vastness of the ocean, unaware of what is lurking in close proximity.

I pulled open the kitchen drawer and armed myself with a meat cleaver. *There is someone else in this house.* I was disorientated. I hadn't sobered up yet and being half-cut didn't make things any easier. *Can I trust my own mind?* I had, after all, consumed a barrel of whiskey the night before. The Devil's water has been said to drive people nuts, but my gut was roaring, it wasn't the alcohol fucking with my mind.

With Luna cradled in my left arm like a new born baby, the cleaver raised high above my head in the other hand, I made my way out to the hallway. The laminate flooring cooled my feet. I had no time to mess around looking for slippers. *Bare feet will have to do, bare feet are better for sneaking around on.* Again, I turned on the hall light as soon as I reached the switch. I stood there for a moment, silent. The only thing I could hear was my own racing heartbeat ringing in my ears. *Boom-boom, boom-boom...*

I edged down the hallway on my tiptoes. When I reached the bottom of the stairs, I looked up into the static black – it chilled my blood. The dream about the demon-goat played in my mind, although the roles were reversed in this version of events. I was now the beast at the bottom of the stairs. I faced the decision: ascend the stairs in the dark, unaware of what may be lurking around up there, waiting for me to fall into a trap, or flip the switch at the bottom of the stairs and illuminate the whole place like a Christmas tree?

I thought about the wretched creature staring into my eyes when I illuminated the stairwell with my Power Rangers torch. Did such beasts roam the earth in *real* life? Were all the nightmares in the world true, the monsters under the bed that most kids describe at least once in their young lives? Had we, in adulthood, come to ignore such vile creatures by sheer choice, pushing them into the realms of fiction?

My heart sank as I hit the lights. I was certain I would be faced by a howling beast, but there was nothing. No howling beast. No monsters. Nothing, with the exception of a slight buzzing sound coming from the golden light bulb.

I wouldn't be able to settle for the rest of the night if I didn't investigate. I was a lot more courageous now that I had rid most of the house of darkness. I lowered the cleaver to my side. My heart slowed back to normal rhythm. *Am I losing my fucking marbles here?*

The light bulb flickered on the top landing as I placed a foot on the first step. I continued to the second step and the bulb flickered again. I stopped. The same thing happened on the third step. Luna was distressed.

The hairs on the back of my neck stood to attention. A tingle trickled down my spine. The bulb sparked again on the fourth, fifth, and sixth step. The bulb went wild on the seventh step, flickering on and off in violent bursts, then stopped.

Luna wriggled free from my arms and landed on her paws. She arched her back and released a prolonged *hiss,* teeth bared and all, scaring the living shit out of me. 'What is it?'

The sound of my voice didn't phase Luna at all. Her eyes were wide, tracking the empty space in front of her. Something had her attention. The way Luna was acting freaked me out, even more so when she sprang forward, swiping at the air with her claws, defending herself from some unknown entity.

I have read stories in the past about cats being able to see into other dimensions. I always thought it was hocus-pocus, but Luna was distressed and interacting with empty space. I believe animals have a deeper connection to the world in some way. I also believe animals can sense an approaching threat. Luna was defending us.

I continued up the stairs until I reached the top. Immediately after reaching the top of the stairs, Luna darted by my feet, down the landing, and into the study. I made my way into my bedroom as it was the closest room to me. There was nothing out of the ordinary. No crazy naked guy hiding out in the bathroom either.

I questioned what I heard, if anything at all; antidepressants, whiskey, beer, anxiety, and tiredness is a great mix in the bag to get the mind tricks fired up. After all, I've had similar experiences in the past. On occasion I was sure I was awake when, in fact, I was fast asleep in my bed.

There was only the study left to investigate. My

eyes wanted to close. I was exhausted. As I was about to walk out of my room, the voice returned.

'Mortem!'

The voice was demonic and blasted with sheer force and aggression. My whole body turned to a mass of jelly as I stumbled backwards, tripped, fell, and dropped the knife. The knife rattled across the floor, scraping and slicing through my brain. I pulled my knees up to my chest, covered my ears with my hands, and closed my eyes as hard as I could. *This isn't real. This can't be real. Wake up, wake up you bastard!*

I rocked back and forth and I was certain in that moment I was going to take a heart attack, convulse, and die right there on my bedroom floor.

I'm not entirely sure how long I was rocking back and forth on the floor with my eyes closed like a child, but it seemed like a lifetime. I didn't want to open my eyes in fear of what I may see, for there was someone, or *something* in the house with me. I couldn't make sense of it in my head. *What the fuck is happening to me? Had the beast from my dream figured out a way to cross over to my world to claim me?* The questions kept rolling around in my head, more ludicrous by the second, burning my brain to pulp.

If someone was to tell me a story like that, even a week beforehand, I would've laughed. Now I have experienced an encounter of my own, something beyond belief – a mighty force was at work. Though my encounter wasn't with what you might think.

When I arrived home that day I could sense someone watching me, my every move. My gut feeling was right on the money.

I was lost in fear and time faded away. Violent images flashed around in my mind. Images of blood, death, and destruction – a show reel of a morbid nature. My mother playing the lead role, dead on the floor and all. Images of me slitting The Troll's fat throat. Christy falling down the stairs and breaking her face. I kept my eyes closed the whole time, my mind was out of control and there was nothing I could do to stop the overthinking. Images seared into my mind, brain tattoos of doom.

The voice never came again, but I heard it loud and clear; the prominent narrator of the sick movie playing on repeat in my mind. I tried to open my eyes a few times, they were glued over. And then I was gone.

RISE AND SHINE

There was a beam of sunshine shooting through the blinds in my bedroom, warming my face. For a second, I was unsure of my surroundings. I stood up, still a little confused as to how I ended up sleeping on the bedroom floor. My head was banging – there was a miniature army inside my head, pounding away with a thousand tiny hammers. The hangover was brutal. My Saturday was ruined, not that I was planning on doing anything in the first place.

I got to my feet, stretched out my arms, and arched my back. My bones were aching, my muscles were stiff. And then it all flashed back in my head, though the fear had left me. The previous night's events seemed like a dream and, the more I considered it, the more I convinced myself it was all an intense, vivid nightmare.

I was a different person when I woke up. The usual anxious sickness in my gut was gone. I wasn't as depressed as usual. There was an endless void in my stomach I no longer had a care in the world – a crushing burden lifted from my shoulders.

I couldn't piece it all together coherently; my mind was struggling to deal with any strenuous thought processing due to the headache. All I wanted to do was get in the shower, freshen up, and eat. I was ravenous. All I could think about was food – bacon, maybe some eggs, and a black coffee with lots of sugar to shake off the cobwebs.

I made my way into the bathroom and undressed. My body was sticky and I smelled like a wino bum. I caught a glimpse of myself in the full length-mirror. I had lost weight, a considerable amount of weight without noticing.

They say people suffering from depression don't recognise these things. I'd be inclined to agree. I couldn't remember the last time I weighed myself, if ever. My ribs were protruding, my biceps thin, and my face was looking gaunt and hollow.

There was a vigorous growth of stubble on my face. My hair was wild and out of control; a large curl flopped down over my forehead, but I was no Elvis Presley. The bags under my eyes made me look more like a haggard old man.

I figured I had to start taking care of myself, eating a sufficient and balanced diet, going to bed earlier to get a healthy amount of sleep, and consuming lower quantities of alcohol. I double underlined the drinking part in my mental notes— then scored it out with my eye-Sharpie.

I didn't ever look at myself in the mirror, mostly because I hated myself and didn't care much for the reminder of how much of a loser I was. That morning was different. I was surveying myself with fresh eyes. I still didn't care much for the person in the mirror staring back at me, but at least I had acknowledged the obvious problems that I needed to fix, which was a start.

I climbed into the shower and turned it on. The stream of warm water on my face was invigorating.

I felt every single drop as it fell upon my skin – a simple, glorious luxury. I often take the simple things like showering for granted.

The velvet lather built up on my head, infused with the scent of pomegranate and lychee. (Herbal Fucking Essences.) Why hadn't I noticed these minor details of life before?

When my mood is high I'm often manic. A few days later my whole world comes crashing to the ground once again with an unapologetic bang. That may well have been the case, the reason why I was so chirpy. *I better enjoy this while it lasts,* I thought.

I am more creative and productive when I'm manic. I get ideas for stories and I spend hours bashing them all out on my typewriter in the study with hopes of having something coherent at the end of it. I tell myself, every time, *this is my masterpiece.* I always fall back down the rabbit hole in the end.

The depression steals my creativity and all the positivity is sucked away by the drain. I stand there and watch as my good intentions swirl away down the plug hole, vanishing with the sewage, turning to shit. And then I'm back to square one, history repeating itself over and over again – Groundhog Day for manic depressives.

This is the way my life has always played out and I know it will be the same old story forever. I made peace with it a long time ago. I wasn't destined to change the world for the better. I never expected to make a mark on this world anyway, just another shit stain in the sea of excrement.

Life has a funny way of playing out. Things can happen in life that you never imagined could happen to anyone, least of all you. Extraordinary things. Things that only materialise in your deepest, wildest, lucid dreams.

I stayed in the shower for two hours that morning. When I eventually climbed out, the whole place was steamed up and looked more like a sauna than my bathroom. I grabbed a towel and wrapped it around my waist, tucking it in at the top.

I picked up my toothbrush, squeezed out some Aqua-fresh onto the bristles, and brushed. Again, the sensation of the everyday task was heightened. The tickling of the bristles on my gums was alien to me. I brushed and brushed, much longer than I usually would. I spat the foamy toothpaste from my mouth, turned on the tap to rinse it away, splashed some water into my mouth, and spat again.

The mirror was foggy and, as I wiped it with my hand, I could have sworn there was another face looking back at me – a face that wasn't my own, if only for a moment. I pulled off my towel and gave the mirror a more thorough wipe down, making sure I got rid of all the streaks. I opened the door to let the steam escape from the room, went back and wiped the mirror again, and kept wiping until it was clear of condensation. When I looked in the mirror for the second time, all I could see was my own face. The steam had skewed my reflection.

I was transfixed by my face in the mirror when Luna came running into the bathroom, scaring me half to death. I had forgotten to feed her before showering, she must have been as hungry as I was. After feeding Luna I noticed the time on the clock.

I was shocked – 1:04PM. I must have slept for quite some time. I took the amount of time spent in the shower into consideration. The day was getting on and my stomach was rumbling.

I fried bacon, sausage, and some mushrooms. I sliced a beef tomato in half to add to the pan for a couple of minutes at the end. I also brought a pot full of water to the boil, added salt, pepper, and carefully cracked an egg into the eye of the vortex I created with a fork.

Poached eggs are the best of all the eggs, and getting them just right was an art that I had spent some time on perfecting – a bad poached egg is all it takes to ruin my day. I don't understand why people would freely choose to destroy their perfectly poached eggs by placing them on top of avocado, fucking avocado. Pineapple on a pizza is another culinary insult, there's just no need for that kind of foul behaviour.

Anyway, I sliced a bagel and slid each half into the toaster. The golden-brown bagels popped up a few minutes later and I added a thick helping of Lurpack butter. Mouth watering. I poured a mug of black coffee and placed it on the kitchen table and sat down to tuck in. My taste buds tingled as I savoured the warm food in my mouth – it was delicious. I hadn't been excited about food in a while. A fried breakfast was a great choice and it hit the spot.

I cleared my plate in five minutes. I washed it down with a good old mouthful of coffee. The strange thing was, after I had devoured my food, I was still hungry. I poured a large bowl of Sugar Puffs and shovelled them into my mouth immediately, the sweetness dancing on my tongue. Everything tasted spectacular.

THE FUNDAMENTALS OF CRUNCH

After I had demolished the Sugar Puffs in true Honey Monster fashion, I opened a packet of Ginger Nuts. I ate four, dunking each one into my coffee. Dunking Ginger Nuts is something I enjoy doing to this day. I've dunked a lot of biscuits in my time, but Ginger Nuts dunked in coffee is the best combination so far. You need to get it right; its all about the fundamentals of crunch. You want a good solid biscuit that doesn't get too soggy.

When my hunger was finally satisfied I sat there for a moment enjoying the silence. I had the urge to get out and about that day. I wasn't sure where I would go, all I knew is that I wanted to get in my car and drive. And that's exactly what I did.

DANDELION AND BURDOCK

The sun was blazing in the cloudless sky. I grabbed a couple of mixed discs before I left the house; Joy Division were singing about how love will tear us a part and all and I was driving, just kept driving with no particular destination in mind.

There's something exciting about getting out onto the open road and cruising aimlessly. I often fantasised about buying a camper van and vanishing from existence – travelling the world, taking each day as it comes, living like a vagabond. What was holding me back? The anxiety and depression. The fear. I was set in my ways and the idea of such a mammoth change was daunting.

I read books written by people who followed their dreams, leaving it all behind. Kerouac's *Lonesome Traveler* always springs to mind. I envy the courage to do such a thing. At that moment in time, I figured the image I had in my head would only ever be a fantasy.

I did, however, have a Supertramp living inside me, waiting to get out. He yearned to be set free, to no longer be caged and surrounded by his own filth like an old imprisoned crow.

They say, *Do one thing each day that scares you.* As I was driving that quote popped into my head like a light coming on, sparking the way in a deep dark tunnel – it may have only been a microscopic light at the time, but it was a light all the same. *Who knows, escaping could be good for me,* I thought. *For my fragile mental health.*

Was it possible that staying alone in Glasgow, wallowing in self pity and being surrounded by so many unhappy memories, was making me progressively worse? Each day stealing another slice of my mind, tainting it with twisted thoughts of violence, suicide, and blackness?

I'm surprised I didn't crash my Jeep. I was lost in wonder – the tarmac pulling me along, the road signs nothing but green flashes as I sped by. Time was lost. I paid attention to the next sign – OBAN 45M. I had gravitated towards Oban and I knew my subconscious was at work. I continued following the signs, my mind eager to relive old memories.

My mother had taken me to Oban a lot during the summer holidays when I was a kid. We always stayed in this old cottage with a coal fire burning. There's something comforting about a coal fire at night – the dancing flames, rustic sparks, and the soothing melody.

We didn't rely on Sky television programmes or Netflix for entertainment back then, and there was no internet to get in the way either. I miss those times a lot. We used to go on adventures, make our own entertainment, and play board games; Ludo, Frustration, Snakes and Ladders, Draughts. My mum had even taught me how to play chess when I was ten.

I had a hard-on for Scrabble. I couldn't get enough of it. My mum used to let me win, but after a while she said she actually had to start trying harder because I was getting so good at it. I'll never know if she was still going easy on me. I did enjoy winning now and again though.

There were twenty or thirty cottages spread around the little village of Ellenabeich. I think that's what made it such a special place to visit – it was isolated, in a good way. Most people kept themselves to themselves. The more we visited, the more people we got to know. We always visited the highland shops. People handed out free tablet and shortbread on a silver serving tray – that kind of thing is exciting when you are a child.

The sky was exceptional during the summer at Ellenabeich. The stars were out of this world – far brighter, piercing through the black velvet. My mum said it's because we were closer to Heaven. And the moon, the moon was at least double in size, emitting a glorious white glow. If you stared at the moon for an extended period of time, it looked like it was slipping closer and closer to earth. I was positive if I stared for too long the whole damn thing would come crashing down, destroying everything in its path.

Everything was made from slate. The village had even been dubbed 'Slate Village'. We'd often wander down to the beach and comb the shore for hours, exploring to see if we could find anything interesting.

There was no sand, only a sea of blue-grey slate mimicking the ocean. Every now and then, I'd find shards with pieces of gold encased. I later discovered that it was called 'fools gold', but my mum informed me at the time it was real, and she'd tell me I'd be rich by the end of summer if I kept finding it.

And then there was the stories, the never ending stories about vikings, pirates, sirens, banshees, and even ghouls. My mum told tales of pirates sailing all the way around the world to get to the secluded shores of Oban to find hidden treasures. I fancied myself to be a fantastic pirate, for I was great as seeking out the fools gold like a magpie – anything shiny and it was straight in my pocket, and my trousers would droop down from the weight of my loot. We once visited a pirate graveyard full of headstones with skulls and crossbones.

When I got older, I found out there was actually some truth to the pirate and viking stories; my mother had just twisted the truth to make the stories more glamorous and cartoon-like for my young mind. She certainly didn't inform me about the raping and pillaging.

The best memories of my life were had on those trips. However, there is one thing that scared me, still imprinted in my mind. An eerie encounter that I couldn't make sense of – there was never an explanation. When I asked about it the expression on my mother's face would change, the look of dread. I guess the scariest things in life are the things we least understand.

We were setting off on an adventure in the mountains. They weren't exactly mountains, more like rocky hills, but they looked like mountains to me. Mum made a picnic – turkey and cucumber sandwiches, dandelion and burdock to wash it down.

We were geared up with our boots on, walking canes in hand – we made the canes from thick branches the night before, peeling off the bark and all. (Every kid loves a big stick, it's natural.) We ventured out into the wilderness. The sun was beating down but we kept moving in the heat, through the long grass and fern, climbing steadily towards the peak.

I had conquered the world when we reached the peak. I was tired and hungry, though I enjoyed the sense of achievement. The view from the top was spectacular. We could see for miles; the sun splashing down on the ocean, sparkling like a layer of blue sapphires dancing atop the sea.

Time stood still as if we were always going to be. I wish I cherished those moments a lot more at the time, the simple things like eating a sandwich with my mother. Never in my wildest dreams could I have predicted her checking out as soon as she did. I miss her voice dearly. I miss her losing at Scrabble for me.

And these are the things that torment my mind each day. Skipping over and over again like a decaying Buddy Holly record, burning my mind alive. Suicide was my eject button if it ever got too much, the easiest way to stop the record, but people don't understand suicide, can't grasp the idea. Suicide takes guts and a clear mind. It's not like *they* would lead you to believe, that it's the 'coward's way out'. Some people are misunderstood and never manage to fit in anywhere. I can feel it. I reckon some people feel it too much. That's the real problem – feeling too much in an emotionless world.

My thoughts get me into trouble and make me feel sad as hell. *Where was I?* We were at the top of the rocky mountains, marvelling over the greatness of the ocean. Before we stood up, I already knew it was going to be a hard grind getting back down to earth; my feet were sore and I could feel a migraine clawing its way in through the base of my neck.

'C'mon, slow coach. The first one back gets to pick the film, deal?' Mum would say.

The incentive of picking the film pushed me harder. On a few occasions, when she let me win, I was allowed to watch the 18 rated films. I was eager to get my eyes on *From Dusk Till Dawn,* and that was the film that pushed my arse to the bottom of the hill – I wanted to witness Sex Machine in action. I mean, who wouldn't want a mechanical penis gun hidden between their legs?

Blisters bubbled at the heels of my feet, my head was pounding, and I couldn't wait to get back to the cottage. My mum was a great motivator and she pushed me, sometimes beyond my capabilities, but we always got there in the end. And for a woman so depressed and close to the edge, she had a quality sense of humour. No matter what, she could put a smile on my face. That's what made the journey home bearable. Her humour spread like wild fire and it was impossible not to get caught up in the flames with her glowing smile and rosy cheeks.

Sex Machine was the last thing on my mind when we reached the bottom. I was too tired to care. The night was a thief and had claimed the summer day, but it was okay – even the world has to sleep.

As we walked home by the water, the sea of slate, and by the pier, I felt lonely. There was something missing, like the universe had shifted, a magnet pulling my happiness from the pit of my stomach. I couldn't explain it, so I didn't try.

MEN IN CLOAKS

I could see a roaring fire out on the beach in the distance, six or seven people gathered around the fire in a ring, all dressed in hooded cloaks. As we approached, a sinister chanting filled the air. There was a carcass on a pole and it looked like that of a ram.

Mum grabbed my hand and pulled me along the road. Her stride had picked up pace and I could sense the panic radiating from her heart. One of the hooded men raised a bony finger. He pointed at us as we hurried by.

'Non believer's blood runs cold!'

Mum warned me not to look at them but I couldn't help staring. The guy was missing his left eye. His right eye looked as though it was made from silver. I've fabricated the fine details in my mind, no doubt – I was an imaginative child – but I could have sworn his skin was scaly, his teeth long and rotten like that of Nosferatu.

'What are they doing?' I asked.

'Nothing, just ignore them.'

I asked her once more about what they were doing to the carcass, she gave me the angry eyes, and I let it go.

The men in cloaks chilled me to the core. There was a dreadful energy surrounding them and I could tell that they were up to no good, but I was too young to understand. My mum isn't here to back up my recollection – the version I remember still gives me the heebie-jeebies.

When we got home to the cottage I was absolutely done. My whole body was aching. It had been a good day; we laughed a lot, got to see some stunning views, and encountered a few chanting maniacs. I got to pick the film. I choose to watch *Bambi* and I'm not even afraid to admit. I loved that movie for some reason. Fucking *Bambi*.

OLD ROADS

ONE MILE read the next road sign. I was in a trance for the duration of the journey.

I went to the old cottage we used to visit, out of curiosity, to see if it was still there. It was. The roof had long caved in and the door was now red instead of green. So many memories lived in that little cottage and it made me sad to see it in such a state. Ferns and ivy had taken the place over. I knocked anyway, caressing the wood on my knuckles.

The village was like a ghost town. The whole place was dead and decaying and it was hard to imagine ever being there. I wandered down to the old Post Office to see if the same woman worked there. She was about ninety in the past and I guessed she was long dead.

The Post Office was closed down. I thought about all the letters once posted in the box; tales of love, sorrow, joy, devastation, and well wishes.

The old village of Ellenabeich had devolved beyond repair. However, she had called me home and I answered.

After leaving the cottage, the idea came to me to go and visit the incredible gaping hole in the world — it was once a quarry, now a huge crater filled with milky-green water. Rocks like shards of metal surrounded the whole thing. I wasn't aloud to go there alone when I was kid – a young girl had fallen to her death and my mother was worried that I'd follow the girl's horrifying fate.

As I stood at the edge, I figured the drop was at least 150 metres. For a split second, I had the urge to throw myself over the edge. I didn't, of course, but I wanted to. I was curious to find out how long it would take a human body to fall to the water below. However, if I jumped to find out, I would no longer be here to document my findings, rendering my suicidal experiment obsolete.

I settled for looking down at the water – it was inviting. I wouldn't blame a single man for wanting to take his shoes off to dip his toes in. The place is lush.

I didn't know it at the time, but that mystical pool of water was to play a huge part in my life over the following weeks.

STANDING CLOSE TO THE EDGE

I swayed on the edge for a long time. Nothing was the same. I was standing inside an ancient painting and everything was so far away from real life.

My mother was fertiliser and the world was

rubbing salt in my wounds. I would have given anything to have my mother back right then – to hear one of her pirate stories, to see her glowing face when she cracked up at her own jokes.

Twenty minutes later, I was back in my car. I had a lump in my throat. I wished this place didn't exist – it was making me weaker than I already was. I didn't need old memories eating away at me. What was the use in them anyway? Old memories only ever made me feel horrible. I'd burn them all if I had the ability to do so.

No. No going back, only forward. Onwards and upwards. There had to be a reason for me being here. Something big was flooding in, curdling in my gut. Was I the next great artist of my time and just unaware? Was I going to write the book I've been talking about for most of my life? Probably not. There was something darker brewing away inside me—something deranged and unnatural.

PEDAL TO THE METAL

I lit a cigarette to calm my nerves and it was swell. I hadn't smoked all day. The cancer danced into my lungs and I enjoyed the thick fogginess of it all. I puffed and puffed as the smoke seeked refuge in every cranny of my anatomy.

My feet were like lead as I pulled away. I never wanted to visit Oban again. I told myself there was an evil in the air here. Only darkness could be had in such a desolate landscape. *What do people even do here?* I thought.

I was lonely on the road. I had that out-of-body sensation again, like I was being watched, and it made my skin crawl, so I stepped on the gas and got out of there. I didn't encounter one single person on my trip to Oban, it was odd. *Am I really here?*

The journey home was like a dream – the roads smooth, the traffic minimal. Luna popped into my head and I wondered what she was doing. Maybe she was chilling out with Goat, or grooming herself. I hadn't been paying her as much attention as I should have been. Life was a hectic drag. Battling your own mind is a tiring expedition.

HOME SWEET HOME

I was glad when I pulled up in the driveway. The sound of the stones crunching under the tyres was hypnotic and eased the knots in my soul. I knew I was in the exact moment in time that I was supposed to be in. Luna by my side. The furball saved me. *It's about time I loved her more.*

As I opened the door she was there to greet me, she always was. I picked her up and nuzzled her into my neck.

'Did you miss me?'

She didn't, but I took comfort in telling myself that at least someone in the world relied on me.

I made my way into the kitchen and fixed her some food and water. The nostalgia of the trip had made me hungry. I sandwiched two large chunks of cheddar cheese and cucumber between seeded bread, added mayonnaise, then a dash of black pepper from the grinder. The bread and cheese was welcomed by my stomach. I made coffee, thought better of it, and poured myself a glass of whiskey instead, smashed it, poured another.

Is this how it is always going to be? Living life as a drunken mess? Wouldn't it be better to just end it all? I thought. Then I remembered it was soon to be Monday and the start of my new role at the cinema. I wasn't looking forward to it at all, but it was just another annoyance on the list of things to deal with it. Either that or go hungry.

A lot of people ask me where my money comes from, it's a simple story. My mum had a life insurance policy. The money turned up in my bank account on my eighteenth birthday. I guessed it would one day die out, so I got a job. Not many youngsters have enough disposable income to buy a Jeep and a house – I bet you were already questioning that?

Yes, I did have my own home and my own car, but the car was getting on and the house was only a one bedroom with an office, located in a shitty area.

I'm surprised the house has only been burgled once at this point. I'd kill anyone who dared try again. I've not got much worth stealing in the first place, besides my soul, if that's even still in there. I'm not entirely sure it ever was.

All I wanted to do after my sandwich was get into bed, and that's what I did, dragging the whiskey with me. I needed to sleep the world away. Luna had mastered the art of stealing pillows. I had to smile at her.

'Who was stupid enough to let you go?'

I'd ask her, but she never replied. I would have died on the spot if she did. The world would be a much better place if animals could talk.

SUNDAY MORNING

When I crawled out of bed in the morning, I was fresh as a daisy. I had nothing planned, so I stayed in all day long. I watched a lot of pornography. I masturbated at least four times over the girls I'd never experience. I loved them all. Every colour, shape, size. Everything got me off. I swear to God, I loved them all. And I'd love them all for real if they let me. I'd love them all equally.

The sun was shining outside, but I was happy to view the day passing me by from the comfort of my own home.

I made roast potatoes, roast beef, Yorkshire puddings, carrots, and peas for dinner, topped off with gravy. Luna experienced her first Sunday roast with me and I treated the meal as a celebration to her good health – I even charged a glass or two in her name.

THE COLOUR PURPLE

Monday arrived. I wasn't too optimistic about going to work that day, but it had to be done. I groaned my way out of bed and dragged myself into the shower. After I had showered I felt a lot better. They say change can do you good. I tried to keep an open mind on the subject of my new job. I wasn't convinced. I shamefully pulled on the sickening purple shirt, demoted from the all-black I was used to.

As I was about to climb into my car, I tripped and cut my knee. There was no time to go back inside to clean myself up, so off I went with a gaping hole in the right leg of my trousers, blood pouring out of the fleshy wound in my knee, gravel and all. *Fucking great,* I thought, hobbling into the car.

I started her up and sped off down the street, annoyed and full of anxiety about the day ahead. Sometimes I think it would've been better if killed myself that Tuesday night in August, the afterlife may well have been slightly more bearable.

ROBYN FOXX

The outlook was dismal. On arrival, however, the possibilities were endless. The excitement in my gut was all too real. For as I made my way through the entrance of The Box, there she was, standing around outside the office door like a lost soul.

She was wearing her head scarf. The same one she was wearing in Asda. I knew that the girl in the foyer was Karen's niece, Robyn.

I limped along the carpet, struggled up the four stairs, and shuffled over to the office door. And that's the first time I finally put a face to the mysterious girl I had been thinking about the last couple of days. She noticed my struggle,

'You okay there?' she asked.

'Yeah, I'm fine, thanks.'

'Are you sure? Looks like you've done yourself an injury.'

She pointed to the cut on my knee.

'Well, I managed to fall over this morning when I was getting in my car. I never had time to change. If I changed I would have been late and then The Troll would have been on my back again.'

I rambled.

'The Troll?'

'Yeah, her real name is Erin but she—'

'She looks like a troll?'

I liked her sarcasm, it was an attractive trait to have and she pulled it off with a delicate charm.

'I'm guessing you're the new girl then?'

'Indeed I am, Robyn.'

Robyn extended her hand. I reached out my own hand to meet hers for a shake.

'Freddy.'

Her hand was softer than Luna's fur. *What moisturiser does she use to keep her skin in such good condition?*

I wanted to kiss the back of her hand and feel her skin on my lips – an inappropriate gesture for the mood of the scene.

My heart was full of moths and I drifted away for a second. She was Rose and I was Jack and there *was* enough room on the raft for the both of us—

'Nice to meet you...I think I'm actually working

with you today?' Robyn said.

God finally decided to show up to the shindig.

'I'm not sure yet. I was a projectionist, but they changed me over to ticket sales on Friday. So this is kinda my first day as well.'

'Ah, cool. I've knocked on the door a couple times. I don't think there's anyone in there.'

She said. I could tell she was nervous.

'Don't worry, they take forever to answer sometimes. I always feel like they're watching me on the CCTV to see how long I'll stand here.'

'Really? That's creepy like.'

I knocked on the door again, put my head down, and continued to wait. I wanted to observe Robyn but it would've been rude, considering she was standing right next to me and all – it would make her uncomfortable. I had to play it cool. I didn't want her to think I was a weirdo before I even got the chance to know her.

As we were standing there, I got a shot of Robyn's perfume in my nostrils. I couldn't help myself,

'What kind of perfume are you wearing?'

'Chanel No.5, why?'

'Just smells nice.'

My cheeks were burning and I was turning red and, as I looked up at Robyn, her cheeks were red too.

Chanel No.5. Where had I smelled Chanel No.5

before? And then it hit me like a kick in the balls. I was surprised it had taken me so long to figure it out. Chanel No.5 was my mum's favourite perfume. It was her fancy perfume for special occasions. Solving small mysteries like that gives me a sense of relief, and the perfume thing was annoying me. I was glad I'd gotten to the bottom of it.

'Thank you.'

Angus answered the office door,

'Right on time, Freddy. I see you two have already met.'

'Yeah, a few minutes ago when I got here.'

'Nice one. You two are working together down at the front ticket booth today.'

'Cool.' I said.

'Robyn came in for training on Saturday, but you'll be fine, eh?'

I had done the training when I first started in case they ever needed me to jump on, or if anyone called in sick. There was nothing to it. Everything was touchscreen. You selected the film, the showing, bashed in the amount the customer paid with, and boom – it even told you the exact change to give back.

'Yeah, we'll be fine. Monday doesn't get too busy anyway, everyone is skint after the weekend.'

'That is very true.' said Robyn.

OUR FIRST DAY TOGETHER

Like I already knew it would be, Monday was sound asleep. Usually the days drag by when there isn't much to do, but not that day. Working with Robyn was fun. She was a laugh and was kinda geeky like Karen had informed me. I hadn't been interested in knowing anything about anyone for so long, because I couldn't connect with any other human on the planet. (Life isn't as easy as a porno.)

Robyn was different. She had a brain full of ideas, dreams, and aspirations.

At twenty-four years old, Robyn already had her life set out and knew what she wanted to do with her future. She told me all about her dreams of becoming a professional artist – she hoped that she would one day be good enough to exhibit her own work. I admired her for having such a strong dream. Luck.

When I asked what style of paintings she created, Robyn told me she was experimenting with surreal portraiture. My knowledge on the topic was nonexistent and I liked hearing about the process she went through to create her paintings.

When asked what I had been up to at the weekend, I tried to sound more exciting than I was, so I told her about my trip to Oban at the weekend.

To my surprise, Robyn had also visited Ellenabeich when she was younger.

I brought up the subject of the old quarry and asked her how long she thinks it would take a human body to fall from the top to the water below.

'Well, it depends,' she said. 'Male or female? Height? Weight? You would also need to consider such things as wind pressure and the weather. Did you think about any of that?'

There was a precision in the way she said it. I liked how she thought it through before answering. The old quarry splashed around in my mind a lot in the following days.

Robyn was also a bit of a film buff, making her even more attractive to me. She loved everything to do with movies; she didn't just watch them, she lived and breathed them, was interested in the 'boring' things like lighting and camera angles, cast members, directors, film theory, even film trivia and spotting continuity blunders.

We talked about that kind of stuff for most of the day, serving only a handful of tickets in between. I liked that we shared a passion for old horror movies. I hadn't anyone to talk to about those things, and it was refreshing to be paired up with someone at work who got what I was talking about.

We had a long conversation about the best horror movies; her favourite was the original *Candyman* of

1992. An odd choice. Some girls don't like that kind of thing, or can't handle the gore, but Robyn wasn't like other girls – I was intrigued by her.

Time was a freight train and I had the *Freight Train Blues*. The more I got to know Robyn, the more I wanted to find a magic button to freeze time, if only for an extra hour or two. *At least I'll be seeing her again in the morning.* The shift came to an end without either of us realising it.

'Jeez, where did the time go?' said Robyn.

'I know, that shift flew by.'

'Same time tomorrow then?'

'I look forward to it.'

Robyn smiled a beautiful smile, one crooked front tooth poking out. She waved, stealing the good vibes with her, electricity in her wonderful blue eyes. Before I knew it, I was back to being alone.

I was looking forward to work the next day. I couldn't wait. I'd been making myself ill about the whole thing and everything turned out to be just dandy. I must admit, pushing tickets and wearing a sickening purple shirt wasn't as bad as I had expected it to be. *I could get used to this. A new job, a new me.* I pulled on my jacket and left for home.

THE COLLECTOR

I never watched a film that night. Instead I read a book. *The Collector* is one of those books that took me a while to get round to reading, even though I'd had it for a year or two – sitting on my bookcase, waiting patiently to be read. I opened a bottle of beer, grabbed the book from the shelf, sat down, putting my feet up on the sofa, and threw my head back on a cushion.

The Collector is about a man named Frederick. He likes to collect butterflies and take photographs. That's all well and good but, as I read into the night, the more Frederick was revealed to be a bit of a nut.

I could relate to him in a lot of ways, the main thing being the fact that he was a very lonely, unloved man. His father had died when he was only two years old, and his mother had left him to live with his aunt, uncle, and cousin.

Miranda, an art student that Frederick has a deep obsession with, is oblivious to his existence in the beginning, though he observes the beautiful stranger from afar.

Frederick plays the pools and, not long into the book, he wins a large sum of money. Just over £73,000. Now, most people would invest some of the money, buy a new car, or go travelling—but not

Frederick. He thinks that the money will cement him into the rich community, but the fact that he *wins* the money sinks him ever deeper and out of touch with the real world. He is back to being an outsider.

Frederick purchases a property in the middle of nowhere, and he proceeds to fix up a room with Miranda's favourite art books and the likes—then calmly abducts her and locks her in the room. The whole idea is to get Miranda to fall in love with him.

And so the story unfolds. I won't spoil the ending, but it was a fantastic read. The only thing Frederick ever wanted was to be loved, and to no longer feel alone.

I felt sorry for him, and wondered if I was just as bad as he was, even though I hadn't locked someone in a room against their will. I couldn't help but feel sympathetic towards him, even though he'd committed such a terrible act. But it's true, love will drive you to insanity, maybe not right away, but it will in the end.

I placed the book back on the shelf with a flare of achievement, having purchased it so long ago. I often find that it's the books that take you a while to get round to reading that turn out to be the real page-turners – it's the same with films. Sometimes they don't grab your attention, but turn out to be wonderful when you give it a chance.

My eyes were heavy; I had powered through a whole book in about four hours, which was good going for me, being a slow reader. I couldn't stop flicking the pages. I needed to find out what happened in the end. It goes like this: *One more chapter. One more. Okay, just one more before bed.*

Before you know it, there are no chapters left to read. The book releases you from its grip, although, you go over the story in your head a million times before drifting off to sleep.

IN THE SHADOWS

I was drifting in and out of sleep for a few hours before Luna jumped off the bed and scared the shit out of me. When I opened my eyes the light in the hallway was glowing. I had switched it off before going to bed that evening.

I had come to realise that something weird was going on in my house – or inside me – even if I couldn't put my finger on it. If there was someone coming to kill me, surely they would have put me out of my misery already?

Luna scurried across the bedroom floor, darting down the hallway, and out of sight. I got out of bed and pulled on my dressing gown. As I was already upstairs, I never had the advantage of grabbing a meat cleaver from the kitchen; all I had was a half-full bottle of whiskey. A big bottle like that could give you a nasty injury, depending on where you struck someone with it. I'd be aiming for the head and eyes.

I glitched to the pain of straight whiskey getting in a cut on my face as I picked up the bottle from the bedside cabinet in my room. The smell of whiskey and blood, pouring down my aching face, blurred vision, and screaming.

I made my way out onto the landing and the light bulb sparked like it did before, but I wasn't scared. My head was sober.

'What do you want?' There was no answer.

'What do you want?' I called out once again.

I had a look down the stairs from over the railing, listening for a moment. I couldn't hear a sound. The whole house was silent.

A flinching shadow caught the corner of my eye as I was making my way back to bed. Luna had disappeared, so I thought it was her.

'Luna?'

I made my way down the hall to the study. Luna was always hiding in there for some reason. I figured she'd be sitting in there on my desk, licking her paws. Or maybe climbing up the curtains – an extracurricular activity she had recently taken up. The curtains in the study were shredded to shit.

As I looked through the crack in the door, a jolt struck my nerves – from the crown of my head, to the tip of my toes. I stood there with my face pressed against the frame, peering with one eye.

There was a shadow sitting on the chair at my desk. Luna was where I expected she would be, but she wasn't wreaking havoc on my curtains. She was still, mesmerised by the shadow.

I couldn't pull my eyes away. There was some kind of apparition in there, a goat-like silhouette— horns and all, and Luna could see it. I drew in a large breathe. I was no longer a voyeur. The shadow twisted it's head around and glared at me with bright eyes, raising a long, foggy finger to it's wispy lips, and let out an emphatic whisper,

'Shhhhhh.'

On instinct, I ran into the room and hit the lights – adrenaline pumping through my veins, my heart hammering my chest to pulp. The shadow vanished in the light, as though it had never been there in the first place. But I had seen it with my own eyes, this vile creature of the night. I could feel it seeping into my lungs. Into my head.

I stood there in silence. Luna wasn't startled by the light, she knew it was coming. Instead, she sat there licking her paws as if nothing happened. There was a burning in my brain. My eyes felt dry, itchy. I ran over and grabbed Luna, bolted back to my bedroom, slammed the door, and got back into bed.

I sat upright, processing my thoughts, gripping a half-empty bottle of Highland Earl whiskey in one hand, my cat in the other like a maniac.

Beetles crawled under my skin, scratching, trying to rip their way to the surface, and the spiders ate my brains. I was running from my own anxiety, my own mixed up mind. My guts were cold with fear. A different kind of fear. A fear of myself. A fear that had left me as empty as the creature.

OUR SECOND DAY TOGETHER

I arrived at work twenty minutes early. A record. There was no point in turning up at work early to sit about doing nothing, waiting on your shift to start. But I guess, if you were part of the clique, you had to get in there bright and early to make sure you didn't miss out on any of the hot gossip of the day. If you did, you'd be in danger of being pushed out.

I know all too well how horrible it feels to be pushed to the outer circle. Although I had grown to enjoy it out here alone. I was hoping Robyn would join me, and not turn into one of the vultures.

I was sitting in the locker room, drinking a cup of coffee, when Robyn walked in – also early. She was more beautiful every time I looked at her.

'Hey,' she said, hanging up her yellow rain coat.

'Morning, how're you doing?'

'I'm okay...I don't think any of the other girls like me. I just walked into the staff room and they started laughing at me.'

'I wouldn't worry about it, they're all idiots. They only speak to me when they want to insult me or something, so I sit in here myself.'

Robyn smiled. She perked me up more than the coffee did.

'That's why I came over, I didn't think anyone else would be in here.'

'Great minds and all that.'

'Defo.'

The vultures disliked Robyn, mainly because she was far prettier than the rest of them, but also because she had that intelligent, too-cool-for-school look about her. I liked that about Robyn. She was different in all the right ways.

She took a seat and continued,

'Did you do anything fun last night?'

'Nothing much. Had a beer, read a book. I'm rock'n roll like that.'

Constipation time.

'Me too. I went for a bubble bath with a glass of wine. What you reading?'

'I read The Collector for the first time. I re—'

'I love that book. So good. It's in my top ten.'

'I enjoyed it. I kinda felt sorry for old Fred.'

'I actually did as well, even though he's mental. He just wanted to be loved.'

'Poor Fred—what you reading at the minute?'

'I started reading The Lair of the White Worm by Bram Stoker. Read it before, but I happened to find a copy'n dad's office the other day, so I pinched it. Read it?'

'Nah, I'm a fan of old Stoker though.'

'My dad said he was sedated when he wrote it, had a *Bram* stroke'r something. You know what, I'll bring it in for you.'

'You're probably going to Hell for that.'

'Haven't we already arrived?'

I looked at my watch. Time was cutting into our conversation. I slurped the last of my coffee.

'You could indeed be right—I guess we better get started, serve the Lord of Fire and all that.'

I flared my hands out like an idiot, but she actually laughed as we walked out the door.

'How'd you find your first day anyway?'

'I wasn't sure the cinema was my bag, it was good though. I liked working with you, you seem cool.'

'Likewise. I hate people, so that's a compliment.'

I could feel my cheeks warming, and I had that fuzz-buzz in my stomach once again, as we walked out across the foyer. I was hungry for Robyn.

MORE TO SEE THAN MOVIES

You may not think much happens in a cinema. Believe me, it does. There's all kinds of weird and wonderful people to observe at The Box. A lot of the time you'd expect it to be the kids who cause the trouble, noise, and make the most mess, but the adults are just as bad – sometimes even worse.

There's not a day that goes by when, usually a young mother, is caught putting pick 'n' mix in her pockets, no joke. Then they continue to half-fill a paper bag with sweets, and it cuts down the price as they already have the other half stashed away like a hamster.

The funniest thing is, the customers like that think they are being sly but, nine times out of ten, they get caught. And that look on their faces is priceless. The 'What, me?' look. They begin to argue their innocence, then give in when they realise the game is up. For the sake of a pocket full of gummy sweets, the customer is escorted off the premises and asked not to return

I feel sorry for the kids – they miss the film they've likely been raving mad about all month, for the sake of a few bucks.

I like to watch the people trying to bring in their own food as well, that's a great laugh. They come in all shifty looking, and you can tell they are paranoid about getting caught with the huge bottle of Dr. Pepper and the family sized-bag of Doritos under their jumper. The funniest thing about this, there's no rule saying you can't bring in your own food and drink. The only thing they ask you not to bring into the halls is fast food like McDonald's, KFC, fucking Nando's; crap like that stinks the whole place out, so it's understandable.

Then you have the people who can't seem to piss straight, or find the decency to park their arses on the toilet pan before taking a dump. I'm certain it's kids in their early teens, trying to act smart in front of their friends, that are the main offenders here—but I did once witness a grown man squatting down and taking a shit in a polystyrene cup, so I'm not sure.

The bathrooms can get in a right state. I'm thankful I'm not the person responsible for dealing with that...shit. There's no way you'd catch me in there with my Marigold-clad hands, not a hope in hell.

The incident with the guy shitting in the polystyrene cup is an unbelievable story. The remake of *The Thing* had been running for forty minutes or so, and was getting into the beef of things. I happened to look out the glass viewing screen from the projection room, and I noticed this guy walking out onto the middle of the aisle, cowering down like he was out hunting rabbits, or something of the sort. He thought he was being stealthy and going unnoticed but, believe me, no matter what you do in life, there's always someone like me watching you from afar.

I was intrigued at first, so I kept watching—and surprise. I could make out the slight glow from his white backside as he squatted down. When it clicked what the dirty old bastard was up to, I shot downstairs, informed Angus what was happening, then ran back up to watch the rest of the story unfold. I was howling to the point of tears, and couldn't wait to see the expression on the guy's face when he was called out for taking a shit in a cup.

The screen lights fired on and, at first, everyone turned round like, *What's going on, we're trying to watch a movie here!*

'What are you doing down there?' Angus called.

The audience followed Angus' gaze, returning their heads to the front of the hall and, there, squatting like a deer in the headlights, the man shitting in the cup was now the star of the show.

He was, of course, escorted from the hall, but not before being insulted, heckled, and violently abused by the angry filmgoers, who were now watching a horror in a hall where a grown man had just released his rotten bowels into a sippy cup.

I was left with one question at the end of that drama—what the hell was the dude planning on wiping with? It would have been more than uncomfortable to sit there for at least another hour with soiled pants.

Anyway, if he only made his way to the toilets like any normal person, he would have missed ten minutes of the film, tops. But as a result of his public disorder, he had missed the full second half and would have to go home and sit and wait on the inevitable DVD release in six months. What a waste.

I'm not sure if that guy ever got charged with indecent exposure or anything, but I do know he was held in the office until the police arrived. I'd love to know what his excuse was when he was being interrogated at the police station. *I didn't want to miss the film.* That kind of excuse wasn't going to cut the mustard, old chappie.

ETHAN HUNT

The first day I got to check the halls with the night vision goggles on, I witnessed a woman sucking her boyfriends cock in the back row. Romance is *not* dead. I took a sick kind of pleasure in viewing the act for at least five minutes – her head bobbing for apples, her man squirming around like a worm in a hot summer sun, preparing to release his junk.

I envied the guy. His girlfriend was smoking hot. I left the hall without saying anything. (Who was I to stand in the way of love's new-age dream?) I let the guy have the happy ending he was looking forward to.

They emerged holding hands when the film was over, flirting, thinking they had successfully pulled off the blowie, unnoticed, like it was their kinky secret. But I knew their secret, and I liked the sense of power – knowing something private got me going.

There's no such thing as privacy in public and, the more I think about it, there's no such thing as privacy, period. They are always watching.

I memorised the peep-show and took a portrait photo in my mind of the girl as she was leaving, so that I could revisit the scene again at a later date. As they left, I didn't think I'd see them any time soon, but I was wrong.

The couple made it a regular indulgence, every Tuesday afternoon. I sold their tickets, so I knew exactly what film they were going to see. I'd let them settle in for a while before investigating for my own sick pleasure. And as sure as hell, every Tuesday, they'd be putting on a different show for dear old Freddy.

My favourite sex scene from the live show was

when she straddled him with her skirt pulled up around her waist, showing her ass and all. She fucked him slowly, grinding in a circular motion on his dick. They had a two hour flick to get through, after all. She looked right at me, smiled, then fucked him a little harder, knowing that I was watching.

Maybe she knew I had been watching them all along. Was I now involved in a secret thing with the girl, or did the guy know as well? I guess I'll never find out, because someone ruined my fun. The couple got busted on my day off by another employee, and were asked never to return to The Box.

People were talking about that for a while. I loved that I had been part of it and knew about it all along. I hoped for another couple to come, settle in, and include me in their public sex game, They never did.

ON THE THIRD DAY

I knew I was going to end up with a broken heart. A heart full of holes, scars, and vulgar burns. But I couldn't stop myself. On the third day, I was almost certain that I was falling in love with the sweet, intelligent, quirky Robyn Foxx.

I've never been a great master of love. I've never even been a great friend to anyone. My heart was a primal beast, hungry and desperate to be satisfied. I loved everything about her, from the way her face dimpled at the corners of her lips when she smiled, to her soft little hands. The smell of her perfume. The way she styled her pixie hair. The petiteness of her frame and her small breasts. The blue and red paint speckled on her trainers.

The question was, did she feel the same way about me? And if she did, what was I to do about it? I wasn't good around people at the best of times. I'd make a fool of myself, no doubt. Do something stupid – say the wrong thing at the wrong time, or even the right thing at the wrong time. Either way, I was in fear of ruining things.

No man can expect to get very far in life by being confined and controlled by the fears scorching a hole in his gut. The creature was living inside of me – of this I was certain – and it was time to suck it up and be fierce.

In the locker room, Robyn handed over *The Lair of the White Worm* and, in return, I gave her a book called *Peephole*

We got along great, never an awkward silence between us; we were on the same page of the same chapter of the same book, right from the get-go.

Robyn could sense what was coming. She went

all shy, playing with her and fidgeting.

I composed the sentence in my mind for a minute, trying to think of the best way to do it. I had only ever asked out one girl in my life, Kat, and look how that turned out. It came screaming out of my mouth a second later, the words taking on a conscious life of their own,

'Do you want to go out with me sometime'

Her face blossomed red petals as she looked down. I thought I was doomed. I prayed Satan was on his way from Hell to collect me, once and for all.

'Sure. I'd like that.'

Her voice was high-pitched and shaky.

I prayed Satan would redirect his journey and go back to torturing souls in the underworld for the time being, for I was in Heaven.

'Really?'

I wanted to confirm and make sure I wasn't hearing things.

'Surprised much?'

She laughed, and I fumbled around with the words on my tongue like a terrible Hugh Grant character. *Just get the words out man.*

'I...I don't ever ask anyone out is all. Didn't want you to think I was a mad weirdo or something.'

I squeezed the sentence from the constipated hole in my face.

'You are weird, but I like it. Also kinda cute.'

Her cheeks had calmed to a pastel shade of pink.

A firework shot off in my chest. I knew it would look pretty at first, but there would be a formidable *bang*, after all the fascination fell from the sky.

What will she think of me when she figures out I'm a crackpot with suicidal tendencies, mummy issues, and a drinking problem? When she finds out I hear voices and chase shadow creatures around my house with weapons? What then? You get your damn shit sorted and deal with it.

We all fall, but it is in our descent that we ascend to our full potential.

TIME FOR A DRIVE

I was in a state of panic when I got home that night. When I was with Robyn, there was this wonderful glowing ball of energy inside me. She gave me confidence, and the best parts of me made an appearance. When she left, however, and I was alone again, I felt anxious, on edge, and the best parts of me retreated into the abyss once again.

What would I wear? What if I dressed too casual and she turned up looking all glam? Or what if I dressed like a Reservoir Dog and she turned up wearing jeans and her paint-stained Converse? What if I Mr Browned myself with the nerves, or ate something that had the same outcome?

Fuck. I should cancel, say I'm ill. But then she'll tell me that she hopes I feel better soon and reschedule. Better to go with it now, get the first date out the way and I'll be able to relax.

The cinema is like my second home, but even I'm not stupid enough to take a girl to the cinema on a first date. It's pointless. You just sit next to them for two hours, in silence, and that's that. We both spent all week in the cinema working, so it'd hardly be romantic, the smell of popcorn and vomit following us around to further dampen the mood.

I also don' t like the idea of going out for dinner on a first date. There's too many things that can go wrong: you either spill dinner down yourself in the first thirty minutes, get food stuck in your teeth, drop your cutlery, or spill your drink all over the girl. And again, spend more time eating than getting to know one another.

I had to think of something better. Something romantic. Robyn said she liked camping, so I hovered over suggesting a weekend camping trip. Then I thought better of it. *Keep it a one day thing. Going away all weekend gives you too much time to fuck up. A day trip? Yes, a day trip is a better idea. That's what we shall do. Go to the seaside and get some ice cream. Every girl likes ice cream, right?*

I didn't know if she was the kind of girl who

would sleep with me on the first date. I didn't know her too well at all, but I was planning on changing that. Anyway, what if she was and tried it on with me? The last thing I wanted to seem like was a fucking virgin, the 'can we wait?' guy. I made a mental note to buy condoms, just in case like.

The only sex I indulged in recently was with my hand, so what if I was like a sack of potatoes in bed? Sprouting out all over the place, mashing into her with no rhythm?

Manscaping – the care and landscaping of the male pubic region – was the next thing I added to my mental to-do list. I really could be doing with some practice. I figured it all out over a neat Scotch, a beer, and a cigarette.

I had been worrying so much that I had completely lost track of time, I looked at my watch – 12:46AM. I was far too awake for bed and needed to let off some steam. I changed out of my sickening purple work shirt, pulled on a mustard cable-knit jumper, some jeans, put on my shoes, grabbed my car keys, and left the house to go for a drive – to clear my head and calm down.

THE CITY STREET LIGHTS

One of the best things a man can do when he is feeling overwhelmed, worried, or claustrophobic, is get in his car, start her up, and drive. This was something I had figured out two years previous. I was climbing the walls one night after work. I was trapped – sick of the sight of the bland interior of my house – so I escaped into the night.

I was driving with the windows rolled down to let the air rush through my hair, and was listening to Iron Maiden on Rock FM. *For the Greater Good of God* was playing as I arrived in the city centre of Glasgow.

The one-way roads in the city are a nightmare for most drivers and, during the day, when the vultures were around, I'd agree. But at night the roads are almost empty – most of the lingering traffic was made up of black cabs, some private hire cars, and buses. And then there was me.

I crawled around the city to see if I could find anything interesting to observe, and it didn't take long until I spotted a girl, half hanging out of a side street, holding a take away, squatting down taking a piss. *Classy lassie.*

I walked past, kicking her in the face with a thick

leather boot. Her jaw dislocated and shot to one side, then swung back again like rubber, shuddered, and twitched for a moment like in the old *Looney Tunes* sketches. The blood sprayed all over the place; rubies shimmering in the moonlight from her nose and mouth, creating an abstract work of art on the white paper her take-away had been wrapped in. She fell to the left and down to the ground, her head making a horrific cracking sound on impact; chips, salad, coleslaw, and cheese raining down on her, covering her vile, bleeding face. I continued driving at 16MPH.

The streets were bustling with party animals and revellers, drunks, brawlers, skunks, and scumbags. This was nothing new to me, but it was busy for an early Thursday morning. Then again, every night in Glasgow is party night.

There's always some kind of drinking promotion on, or live music, or comedy night. In fact, there's an excuse to go out every single night if you really wanted to. (I always wonder where people get the money to do that).

Up ahead, two old guys were having some kind of dispute. I switched off the radio so that I could eavesdrop as I crawled past, hugging into the curb. The guys were arguing about something alien to me, communicating in a dialect fuelled by drugs, alcohol, or both.

'Joe. Fuck. Sake mwwan...'

They pushed each other around, spewing out more incoherent words and slurs. I guessed these two guys were old winos – one was clutching a three litre bottle of the gut-rot, Three Hammers. The other was trying to get it from him – probably the root of the argument they were having.

Both were dressed in dirty denims, scruffy coats, with long, scraggly hair, and beards. It was evident they hadn't caressed their frail bodies with soap or hot water for a while, and were most likely homeless. *The storm will come and wash them all away.* I carried on driving.

I could see tits in every direction. Short skirts, ass, and fake tan—lots of fake tan, streaked over skin like tea stains.

Everything is fake these days, from eyelashes, to teeth; people were even getting arse implants, and not just the girls. The dudes were at it, too, with peck implants, and even hair implants. Fucking parasites. Cancerous growths on the crust of society, true identities crumbling away like ash. Slowly suffocating everyone under them. If I was to ever go bald, which I think is highly unlikely due to the thickness of my hair, I would just shave my whole damn head. There's nothing worse than a bald man with with four strands of hair, trying their best to gel said four strands in such a way to cover their whole gleaming scalp like Gollum. Have some dignity man, shave it and be done with it already.

The city streets were littered with vulturous, consumerist parasites, but the city street lights still danced in a colourful melody. If those fluorescent lights could talk, they'd be able to tell one million tales, never shared. Tales of rape and murder. Muggings, assaults, robberies. Tales of unfaithful husbands and their cheating wives. Of promises forgotten, over-priced gifts, depleting bank accounts, and debt. Tales of things we don't need and things we think we do. Of hangovers and the source of the thousand curdling stomachs the morning after. Headaches and missing teeth, bruised cheeks, and scraped knees. Missing wallets and lost jackets. Tales of copious amounts of hard drugs and overindulgence, of teeth grinding, and profuse sweating. If those fluorescent lights could talk, they could tell one million tales, never shared. And maybe, just maybe, they would have some happy memories too.

Time was a blur, and I was a passenger in my own movie. The protagonist, cleaning up the streets. An invisible taxi driver taking out the trash at the end of a hard night on the grind. Washing blood and sin from my skin with whiskey, and sucking smoke into my aching lungs. Oncoming traffic blinding my eyes with headlights on full beam, bastards. The world was silent now, peaceful; the revellers, brawlers, skunks, and scumbags all silent now. Sleeping in the back streets of the inky black city; hiding in the alleyways with the rats and the sewage, taking refuge from the soon-to-be rising sun like vampires, having just drained the whole damn place of life. Bellies full of sweet blood. Time for sleep now, time for sleep.

The driver behind me brought me back to reality as he honked his horn. I looked in my rear view mirror – his face was rough and full of stubble. I think he was missing his front teeth. He threw up his hands, miming, 'Fucking drive, man.'

I was doing 10MPH, so I slammed my foot on the pedal, screaming away into the night. I honked my horn in retaliation. A few seconds later, the guy with road rage shot past me like a road warrior, soon becoming a star in the distance.

THE GOOD DAUGHTER

The time was 2:04AM. *Ten more minutes,* I thought. *Then I'll head home.* But right in front of me, I could see an interesting situation unfolding. I pulled in at a bus stop, turned off the lights and the ignition, so that I could go unnoticed and observe the conclusion of the story.

Not far from the rear of Glasgow Central station, there was a girl, red hair falling down her back in a blaze of ringlets, leaning into the window of a silver Audi. I'd say she was in her late twenties. I could tell she was a prostitute from the way she composed herself, likely trying to gain some business from the driver of the Audi. She was wearing black fishnet tights and a shorter-than-short tartan skirt. The girl was indeed wearing boots, but they looked like Dr. Martens; not your stereotypical hooker boots that climb up over the knee. She looked as though she may once have been pretty, but now her face looked haggard, plastered with far too much foundation and lipstick.

I ran over to the car and pushed the girl aside – she was wearing cheap perfume and I got a shot of it right in the face. I pulled open the passenger side door of the silver car and pounced on the guy behind the wheel. An insignificant man. Old, unattractive, disguised in a fancy grey suit. I forced my hands around his neck and throttled him. His eyes bulged and he was trying to say something, his tongue all twisted and tied, but I wouldn't let the lowlife get a breath – he'd sucked one too many from the atmosphere already. I pulled out my hunting knife from the inside pocket of my jacket, chibbed him in the jugular with one swift blow. The life drained from his eyes, the violet-blue capillaries popping. He sputtered filth all over me and it made me sick. I pulled the knife from his throat, the blood shooting out in one thin stream, spilling over the dashboard; a red water feature display flourished on the inside of the windscreen. The show only lasted a moment before his head fell forward. He clutched at the gaping wound for another second or two before his life was gone. I got out of the car. The girl was standing by in disbelief. 'He was going to pay me good money, you arsehole!' Ungrateful. *Maybe you can't be saved?*

I came back to life. That was the second glitch of the night, and in a short period of time. They were becoming more frequent, more detailed, more frenzied, violent, and definitely more real than they had ever been before. I refocused, and the girl with the red hair was getting into the car with the unknown driver. As they pulled away, without even realising it, I started up the Jeep and followed them. *Better keep my distance.*

As I trailed behind the Audi, I thought about the girl inside, the acts she was about to perform for a fee, unspeakable acts of degradation. I was curious to what had happened so bad in her life that she ended up on this dangerous path of destruction. This putrid, degrading life was surely going to end up with her being raped, robbed, or murdered. And when they showed her face on the news, nobody would care, because she done it to herself. Yet another cold case that won't be solved until twenty years later when the perpetrator gets picked up for drinking under the influence.

What about her family? Are they dead, or had they disowned her? There has to be a reason for this career choice. I figured the girl was most likely feeding some kind of habit. My money was on heroin; skag has always been a big problem in Glasgow. Skaggies are a different species altogether – they'd inject bleach if they thought it was going to get them off their rocker.

The prostitute I was tailing may not have been a skag-head, she may have had no addiction at all. Some people fall on hard times without ever touching a drug in their lives, just fall through the cracks. And once they are through, they keep slipping deeper and deeper down the hole, the walls chomping in around them with razor-sharp teeth. Believe me, when you fall down the rabbit hole like that, you'll probably never see the light of day again. Though, if you do, pat yourself on the back and award yourself a gold star for effort, for that kind of struggle back to the light must be one bitch of a fight.

If the girl had parents, they would've been worried sick. How did they manage to sleep at night, knowing their beloved daughter was out selling her snatch for buttons? The daughter who was once pure, innocent, good, aspirations and all, with her whole life ahead her.

The Audi pulled down an alleyway. I edged up to the opening and got out of the car. I hugged into the wall, shuffled to the corner, then had a peek to see what was going on. I couldn't see much at all until the car door swung open. The girl got out and walked round to the driver's side.

The guy turned off the ignition and climbed out. He was surprisingly young, short. He wasn't wearing a suit like I had imagined he would be. He looked like a normal person. The guy wasn't ugly, from what I could tell, had a decent build and, of course, a nice car.

He could have been a high-rolling entrepreneur, but wouldn't someone like that pay a little more cash for a high-end escort? I don't know much from the world of prostitution, and most of the knowledge I do have has come from movies, *Taxi Driver* in particular, of course. Jodie Foster playing a fourteen year old hooker and all.

I was a voyeur once again, like the time in the cinema with the young couple. This was more dangerous, risky, and exciting. I was more likely to be caught out on the streets. I fed off the rush of what I was doing. I know it's wrong and disgusting, but I didn't care at all. I got off even more when I thought about how fucked up and wrong it actually was. I watched intently – sucking irregular breaths of toxic, sleazy air. My eyes zoomed in and focused.

The girl was on her knees, her head bobbing back and forth. The guy had his hands on her head, aggressively pushing at her and grabbing the blazing ringlets on her head. I could hear the guy moaning. I bet he liked the thrill of doing it outside, playing with fate, the dirty old bastard.

He grabbed her by the jaw and pulled her up to his face, kissed her on the mouth, then flipped her round, bending her over the side of the car. Her hands were spread over the bonnet, and she heaved and moaned as Mr Audi fucked her from behind. He picked up pace and, after only a minute, he grunted and shuddered. *What a waste of money.*

The guy fixed himself. The girl pulled down her skirt. He pulled some cash from his wallet and paid her. He slapped her on the ass as she walked away, whistled, and climbed back into his car. The Audi reversed from the ally, so I jogged back to the safety of my car, got in, and closed the door.

I let out a cathartic sigh. I had become the uninvited participant in a sexual transaction, and I was satisfied with the peep show I had sat in on for free. I admired myself in the rear view mirror. *You dirty dog.*

The Audi was soon out of sight, as if it had never been there in the first place. The last ten minutes drifted, fusing into the figments of my imagination. The prostitute appeared from the ally – strolling down the road like she was eager to impress a *Vogue* photographer – back towards Central station. I let her get some distance before starting up my car and following her.

I was unaware of my own intentions, if any, but something came over me, telling me to to follow the hooker, so I did. She had a sexy walk, looked great from behind; she may have been beautiful at some point in her life. All the attractive girls from school turned out to be howlers in later life. Maybe it was the same kind of deal with the prostitute.

Without thinking about it, as though it was second nature to me, I had started fishing around my inside pocket and, when I became aware of what I was doing, a euphoric sensation ran through my blood. I had been feeling around for the knife. The knife I used in the glitch. The hunting knife my father passed down to me; it was at home in a box somewhere and I hadn't taken it out in years. The pocket was empty.

I ate the curb. The girl turned around and

stopped. She looked left and right to check the coast was clear. When she was satisfied, she strolled over to my car. I rolled down the window, just like you see in the movies. She leaned in the window. I could smell tobacco on her breath.

'What you lookin for, hun?'

She looked a lot older up close; the crow's feet around her eyes were severe, the wrinkles seeping out onto her lips, the lipstick cracked like dry paint.

'What you offering, and how much will it skin me?' I said.

I surprised myself. I was cool and collected – there was no anxiety and no awkward nerves, sweating, or shakes. None of that stuff. Someone had poured warm honey all over my naked body, although, the peaceful vibe was fading, and excitement clawed my skin. I'd never dreamed of picking up a prostitute before – the thrill of the situation was teasing my heart.

'Do anythin you want for forty quid but I want fifty if you shag m'arse.'

Anything I want? Does that include ripping your throat out and cutting your body up into a hundred tiny pieces?

'Cool, jump in.'

I focused on her throat as she pulled on her seatbelt. *I'd worry more about me than dying in a road traffic collision. My knife would slice through your skin like butter.*

There was a prostitute in my car, something that I hadn't planned on happening, and I didn't know what to do, so I pulled away from the curb, my intentions still unknown.

'So what's it gonna be? Time's money. You want a handjob? Blowjob?'

She was straight to business, rubbing her hand over my inner thigh. I'd be lying if I said I didn't like it; this was the first girl to touch me in a while and it turned me on a hell of a lot. Her hand slid up my thigh and over the bulge between my legs, rubbing back and forth on the outside of my jeans. I couldn't concentrate. I waited until I came to a dark side street, drove down it, and stopped the car – taking a leaf out of old Mr Audi's book.

'Wait a minute, I've never done this before.' I said.

'Sure. That's what they all say. Don't worry, your dirty secret is safe.'

I pulled her hand away.

'Honestly.'

'Why'd you pick me up then?'

There was a moment of silence, stale and awkward.

'Why do you, like, do this?'

'Is this an interview, mate? I do it cause I have to.'

'But why do you have to?'

'To make rent, and am'a fuckin meth head. You

think I'd be doing this if I had a choice?'

'Probably not. Do you enjoy it?'

'This kind of chat gettin you off? Fine. I can be anythin you want me to be.'

She rubbed back and forth on my crotch again, unzipped my jeans, and slid her hand inside.

'Am a durty slut, like bein fucked by strange men and suckin dick.'

An image of her being bent over the car flashed in my mind, although, I was playing the role of Mr Audi. I pulled the knife out of my pocket and, as she was on her knees, I rammed the knife into the side of her throat.

I was brought back to reality when my phone vibrated in my pocket. I took it out and had a quick look. It was a message from Robyn. My heart sank. What was I thinking, pulling over a prostitute in the middle of the night? I pulled the prostitute's hand from my trousers and told her to get out.

'What the fuck's wrong with you? Fuckin freak.'

'Get out my car, this was a mistake.'

I had been trapped in a haze for the last couple of hours, but my phone vibrating in my pocket brought a moment of clarity at just the right time.

'You still owe me for time.'

I figured that was only fair. I gave her the full forty.

'Get out.'

I said, and she did, slamming the door behind her. She put up the middle finger as she stormed off, a harlot in the night, fading away into the dark with all the revellers and the scumbags and the parasites and the vultures and the vampires.

That night was the first time I thought about killing someone for real—and if I had the knife in my pocket, Iwould have cut the prostitute's throat. I was as calm as a cucumber, no feeling of guilt, nothing. The creature inside was taking over, and I liked it.

I opened the message from Robyn, excited to see what it said: HEY, you up? I'm having nightmares and I can't sleep :(xxxx

I replied: Hey, I'm in bed reading. What are the nightmares about? Want to talk it out? Xxxx

I put my phone back in my pocket, zipped my jeans, and headed home.

MIRROR IMAGE

My heart was racing when I woke up on Saturday morning. Today was the day. My very first date with Robyn. The last couple of days had went by in a blur, all I could think about was trying not to mess things up. I was no James Bond and, as we have already established, my track record was definitely shaken and not stirred. I had to keep it cool and not act all edgy and weird. I knew if things went well, Robyn and I could work. The thought of it all was making me feel ill, in the best possible way.

The only person I had to confide in was Luna, and she just purred and nodded. As much as I loved her, she wasn't much help at all.

I had two hours to kill before I had to go and pick Robyn up from her house. I already knew it would feel like a year, watching time hanging onto seconds like each one was made from gold.

Time moves slow for people who wait.

I struggled to fall back to sleep. My mind was too active, so I got up and went through my cupboards to decide what I'd wear. I was lost. I pulled out everything I owned, hangers and all, and lay it all out on my bed. I lay out my shoes at the bottom of the bed and began piecing an outfit together.

Blue shirt, black chinos, and black brogues. Too formal. Mustard chinos, burgundy jumper, brown brogues. Too beige. After standing around in nothing but my boxers for twenty minutes, I settled on the outfit: black skinny jeans, a grey Kurt Vonnegut tee, black Vans Rowley's with white soles. I added a blue denim jacket. *Perfect.* I danced my way into the shower.

For the first time in forever, I sang my heart in

the shower, and it eased my nerves. (It's true what they say, music really does heal the soul.) I had only been in the shower for five minutes when a loud *bang* startled me. I immediately stopped singing, cut off the water, and pulled back the shower curtain. I climbed out, wrapped a towel around my waist, shuffled to the hallway, and looked down the stairs at the front door—as if it was going to open itself. I figured it was the post man knocking, but then I remembered I didn't get post on a Saturday, not back then, anyway.

As I made my way back into the bathroom there was, what appeared to be, a trail of muddy prints along the tiled flooring. *Maybe Luna knocked over a plant pot, hence the bang, and dragged the dirt into the bathroom?* A plausible explanation, but I knew I was rationalising. A cold familiar feeling climbed its way into my stomach.

I walked with caution towards the study. When I opened the door, there was no shadow monster and no Luna. *Please don't do this to me today. Today of all days.* I was mystified when I made my way back to the bathroom and the prints were gone. I continued getting ready, ignoring my own mind, and it worked, if only for a minute.

I visualised what the day ahead was going be like as I brushed my teeth. When I looked up in the foggy mirror, the same thing happened as before;

the reflection looking back through the haze wasn't me. This time the shape was all wrong. I rubbed my eyes with balled fists and proceeded to wipe down the mirror. As the mirror cleared, an image materialized, but it was not me—the goat was standing there.

I took a step back, closed my eyes as tight as I could, fluttered my lashes, and refocused. I felt no fear, I was in awe of what was standing in front of me. The goat was no longer demonic looking, instead, he looked clean. His fur was a grey-white colour, well groomed, and he had a smirk on his face. If that wasn't strange enough, he was wearing a black blazer, white shirt, and black tie. I swear to Christ. He was staring back at me.

I darted my head to the left, he mimicked my movement. I snapped to the right, and he once again moved with me. *What the fuck is happening to me?* My next thought was to grab my phone and take a snap to see if it was real, or all in my head, so I flew to my bedroom, grabbed my phone from the bedside cabinet, and slid back into the bathroom. He was still there.

I raised my phone, fumbling, and fired a few shots. To my astonishment, the goat done the exact same thing, same phone and all. I leaned in, pushing my face closer, eventually pushing my nose up against the glass. The glass did not act as a barrier. My head glided through like the mirror wasn't there at all.

There was nothing but blackness on the other side, dripping like hot tar, the goat standing there in the middle of nothing, dressed in a suit, no longer a reflection, but a full three dimensional figure. We studied each other before he calmly whispered, unlike the demon from my nightmares:

'Everything must die.'

I forced my head free from the mirror. I fell back against the wall with a *thump*. When I looked up the mirror had solidified, and the only reflection looking back was my own. I fumbled with my phone, opening the picture gallery.

One half of me was hoping that I had captured some tangible evidence, but the other half was hoping I hadn't. There is no way I could explain what just happened. People would think I was even more of a creep than they already did.

The only image I captured was an image of myself, looking in the mirror, holding my phone. I was losing my mind, I had to be. I was speechless and confused, but not scared. I realised in that moment, the Goat was no demon from Hell, but my alter ego. A personification of my disease. My very own Tyler Fucking Durden.

GREENLESS GROVE

Robyn stayed in a respectable part of town – 32 Greenless Grove. I always thought it sounded like a fictional setting from a Tim Burton movie, but it wasn't. The irony – lush trees, shrubbery, and flowers were planted in every garden, each garden enclosed with a fancy wooden fence. The houses were all bought and the street reminded me a lot of the American suburbs.

Going 12MPH, I counted down the numbers until I got to Robyn's. She lived in the last house in the corner, and it was huge; three stories, a garage, a large garden, the full works. There was a Black Mazda RX8 and a silver Ford Ranger parked in the driveway.

I knew Robyn still lived with her parents and, judging by the house in front of me, I could tell they were a wealthy family. I turned off the engine and sat there for a moment, fantasising how good her life must have been – growing up in a fancy house with loving parents – and I'd be lying if I said I wasn't at least a little envious. On the other hand, being wealthy doesn't necessarily mean you're happy. I took comfort in telling myself that at the time.

I put my hands out in front of me. To my surprise, I didn't have the shakes. I wasn't even sweating, nothing. I was excited, a little nervous, but I was happy and feeling optimistic about the day. I fixed my hair in the mirror, admired the small beard and moustache I was now sporting, popped a cherry Airwave into my mouth, and stepped out the car.

The air was fresh and I invited it into my lungs with pleasure as I strolled over to the house, through the gate – admiring the Begonias – up to the front door, and rang the bell. The bell made me jump, as it sounded like the old school bells they used to have when I was at primary school. I waited.

I could see Robyn approaching through the glass, she was holding something in her hands. I tried not to stare into the house, but I did.

She opened the door with a smile on her face, stretching from ear to hear.

'Hey, right on time.' Robyn said, locking the door behind her.

'Ha, I got ready too soon. Got bored sitting around. The traffic was quite bad though so it worked out well.'

She leaned forward and put her arms around me, pecking me on the cheek.

'I'm happy to see you, can you tell?'

'I've been looking forward to seeing you as well. I like your dress.'

'Thanks, bought it especially for today.'

She curtseyed and bowed her head. It was a loose-fitting summer dress – peach with a subtle floral pattern. It was a lovely dress and all, but I was more intrigued by the flat, rectangular parcel she had under her arm, wrapped in brown paper, tied with string.

'I don't do dates, so I didn't have a clue what to wear.'

'Well, I think you look good. Your shirt is pretty cool, man.'

'Thanks—what's in that parcel?' I continued, opening the passenger side door of my car to let her in.

'Eh, well, I'll show you later. I'll get embarrassed if I show you now.'

'Ah, was just wondering. Now I'm even more intrigued.'

Robyn climbed into the passenger side, placing the parcel in the back seat.

'Such a gentleman.'

'Of course. I'm old school like that.'

I closed the door over, walked round to the other side, climbed in, and started the engine.

As I checked the rear view mirror, my new friend, Goat, was looking right back at me—the miniature version. I pushed him from my mind, pulled out, and drove away.

THE CURE

One of my favourite places to visit is a little village called Luss, down by Loch Lomond. The water may be murky and the sand course, but I love that place. On a clear day, you can look out over the water and see Ben Lomond in the distance—a spectacular sight.

I would often drive to Luss, mainly to escape the smog of the city for a while and enjoy the scenery. I'd walk to the end of the pier and remember the good times we had as a family when I was young. You were aloud to jump from the pier back then but, after a few intoxicated people drowned, they banned it. Typical, a few scumbags ruined it for us all.

Anyway, I'd stand at the end and imagine sharing the view with the love of my life. I'd tell her to stand against the railings, and I'd snap off a few shots of her with Ben in the background. Her hair would be blowing in the wind and she'd be smiling, sticking out her tongue and winking and telling me she loved me and all. Then we'd get ice cream and hold hands and we'd share vanilla-stained kisses with strawberry sauce, maybe some sprinkles. And I'd hold her, never let her go, and we'd be together forever and I wouldn't be lonely.

When we got out of the city, Robyn started poking around in the glove-box.

'You got any good music for this little trip?'

'Of course, give me a minute, I've got some discs on my side.'

I was trying not to kill us and get a CD at the same time, but I guess Robyn didn't want to die, because she leaned over me and said:

'Just you keep your eyes on the road, Mad Max.'

I could feel her warm body on my thighs as she leaned over—a bigger distraction than looking for a CD. Her dress was thin. Her skin close to mine but not quite touching, the sheer fabric tearing us apart.

Keep your eyes on the road, I told myself. *Focus, you pig.* Goat was in the mirror smirking at me the whole time. I had an urge at that moment to swerve the car into the barrier and kill us all – everything must die. It wasn't the right time for death and destruction—yet.

Robyn slid back over to her side, a handful of discs in her hand.

I made multiple playlists and burned them onto blank discs at home. I'm not a fan of listening to full albums by the same person. I like a mix.

'You have, like, sixteen mixed discs here. What one will I put in?'

I looked at her fingers thumbing through the discs. The nails were painted a deep blue colour, her cuticles were frayed, torn, and the skin was hanging at the base of each nail.

The Sharpie ink was smudged on disc sixteen, but it was my favourite compilation.

'Sixteen is the best one I think, depends on what kind of stuff you like.'

Her slender fingers pulled the disc from the stack and fed it to the player. After a gritty, mechanical chomping, *The Lovecats* bounced into action.

'Ah, I love The Cure! You're a bag full of surprises. What else you hiding under that skin?'

If I was to give an honest reply, I would have said something like: *A horrible, tainted, infectious obsession with violence, and I feel like I want to cut your skin from your body right now, to kill us all, and lay dead with your naked corpse...*

'Me? I'm an open book.'

Lies. Lies. Lies. The mask was secured to my deceptive face.

We smiled simultaneously, and I watched her small lips curl at the sides, like the Joker without the scars. Her smile was not self-inflicted. It was pure, innocent, and perfectly imperfect. The dimples on her cheeks danced inwards, as though she had bitten into a lemon, in slow motion, delicately, and not all sour-faced.

If there was a heaven, this was it. I was blessed and pure on that blooper reel, like her. No longer a waste. No longer evil.

'Well, you're the kind of book I want to be reading. There's something about you.'

Robyn closed her eyes and I viewed her in the mirror, swaying her head back and forth, her legs bouncing in time to the drums of Andy Anderson.

I wanted to freeze that moment forever. Take it home like a Kodachrome picture. Hang it on my refrigerator, but I couldn't. I savoured it, taking in every detail, so that I could revisit the scene at a later date.

SUNSHINE ON A RAINY DAY

I pulled into the car park, twenty yards from the beach, and we climbed out. The sun was beating down, however, I could see clouds forming in the distance. Robyn fixed herself and stretched her legs. I stretched my legs and lit up a cigarette.

The car park was dead, which was good. Too many people on a beach ruins the tranquillity and the beauty of it all. The last thing I wanted to see was some old dear with saggy skin, rubbing factor fifty into the deep crevices on her arms, or even worse, some old guy covered in hair, cutting around the place in his Speedos.

Robyn walked towards me and hooked her right

arm under my left arm, our hands almost touched.

'Where too?'

'This way,' I said. 'Just through the trees.'

'I don't usually go to the forest with strange men, you know, but I trust you.'

'It's not a forest,' I laughed. 'There's a pathway leading down to the beach.'

We strolled arm-in-arm through the trees. We were welcomed with the stunning view of Loch Lomond when we emerged from the other side. Robyn stood there fore a moment, taking in the scenery, a huge breath of air in through her nose, pointing her chin to the sky.

'I can't believe I've been missing out on this.'

'Great view, eh?'

'Yeah, it's stunning.'

'I love this place. The water is freezing, but I used to come here a lot when I was a kid and splash about in it, always ended up with a cold the next day. I guess you don't worry about that kind of stuff when you're a kid.'

'Aww,' Robyn said, then pointed out into the distance. 'What's over there?'

'Ben Lomond. You ever hiked up it? The view from the top is awesome.'

'I can imagine. I've never been down this way before, and I'm sad to admit it, but I've never went on a proper hike before.'

'Really? You can get up that bad boy in about two or three hours, and it's a good day out, great sense of achievement when yo get to the top and that.'

'Maybe we could walk up together sometime?'

My heart skipped a few beats when Robyn said that. The fact she was hinting at a future day trip together was clarification she was thinking ahead.

There's nothing worse than a one-sided love affair. That was never the case with Robyn. The attraction was mutual, we were both on the same page.

'Of course,' I said. 'I'd like that.'

Robyn pulled off her shoes to feel the sand in her toes, and I did the same; even though I already knew the sand was full of stones, but I didn't care. The waves lulled back and forth, occasionally covering our feet as we walked alongside the water towards the pier. We strolled in silence. A comfortable silence. Robyn stretched her arm out, dancing in time with mine and, a second later, our hands were clasped together as one.

We walked along the pier, hand-in-hand, exactly how I had played it out in my head many times before, and I was happy. The happiest I had ever been in my life; my mind was calm and, for once, I didn't feel like my life was useless. We walked all the way to the end and looked over the edge, into the muddy water below.

'Should we jump?' Robyn suggested.

'We used to jump off here all the time, but a couple of people drowned one day, so they banned it. Apparently they put concrete blocks down there to make the water shallow. Not sure if that's just a myth. Best not to find out though, wouldn't want to end the day in the hospital with broken legs.'

'You're right. You know, we didn't do much as a family when I was young. My mum was always out with her girl friends, drinking cocktails or whatever, and my dad was always away on business trips, so a lot of my childhood was spent in the house with the babysitter watching movies, or playing by myself in the garden when the weather was nice. I wish we went on more trips to places like this.'

There was a sadness, a loneliness, in Robyn's voice, and it made me feel strange, but I could relate to her. Like I had already thought, a wealthy family isn't always a happy one.

The more I got to know Robyn, the more I realised her life hadn't been all rainbows and unicorns; she was wearing a mask, just like me. Every once in a while her mask slipped, and I got a glimpse at what was hiding on the other side.

'Let's make up for it, go on loads of adventures together?'

I wanted to make her feel better about her lost

childhood, to comfort her.

'Deal. Why are you so nice to me?'

We made a pinky promise. Robyn leaned back against the railings. The images I had in my head were materialising in real life, before my eyes, so I took advantage. I pulled out my phone.

'Let me take a picture of you with the scenery in the background before the clouds steal the sky.' I said. She went all shy on me.

'I hate having my picture taken. But alright then, let me fix my hair first.'

When she had fixed her hair, she flashed her cute, crooked tooth, dimples and all.

'Say cheese.'

I snapped a photo as Robyn laughed, making the photograph more candid. And when I looked at the photo it was perfect – capturing her spirit and delicate beauty had been no hard task.

'Get over here,' she said. 'If I'm getting papped, so are you.'

She snatched my phone and pulled me in close, our cheeks pressing together. She stretched out her arm to get us both in the photograph – which was the first selfie I had ever been featured in – and snapped. In the first shot, Robyn turned her head and kissed me on the cheek at the last second – I can still feel that kiss on my face to this day, like a lover's branding of flesh

A few more selfies followed. Robyn threw up the peace sign in one, stuck out her tongue in another. I wasn't up to date with selfie etiquette, so I just smiled, and it was a real smile too, not fake, not forced, not constipated – one hundred percent real, a true representation of joy.

I liked how Robyn had a silly side, and that she didn't take herself too seriously – it's a great trait to have. She made me feel like a love-sick teenager, and helped me forget about my troubles. When I was with her, the depression was bearable, and the anxiety was almost non-existent. I was *normal*.

We stood there on the pier, flipping through the photographs. For some reason, in one of the pictures, my left eye was squint, making me look a little like Quasimodo – that was the main source of hysterics.

We were in a bubble of our own, like we were the only two people left on a barren planet—something that I could've lived with. In fact, we hadn't noticed two men holding hands and doing the exact same thing at the other end. They were most likely lost in their own little bubble, and it made me happy as hell.

The clouds soon rolled in, thick and fast, and the cold breeze was becoming more of a wind. We made our way back down the pier to get some ice cream from the van at the bottom. By the time we got there, Robyn was shivering. I took off my jacket and wrapped it round her like a cape.

'Are you too cold for ice cream? Shall we just go back to the car?' I said.

'No way. What kind of person comes all the way to the beach and doesn't get ice cream? That's plain ludicrous.'

The guy in the van was kind of staring at us like we were aliens trying to figure out what planet we were on.

'What can I get you two?'

He was fat with a yellow face, red nose, and was trying to hurry us.

Robyn got bubblegum with chocolate sprinkles. I went for mint chocolate chip. We walked along the beach once again, licking our cones—this time we done so with our shoes on. The sun was gone and the blue sky was no longer visible. The beautiful rolling landscape and Ben Lomond had been eaten by mist in the distance.

The heavens opened, making the whole place look like a melancholy watercolour panting, dripping with anguish.

'Let's get the hell outta here.' Robyn said, pulling my jacket over her head.

We hurried along the beach to the trees, where we took refuge from the rain, soaked to the bone. Robyn's dress was transparent. I could see her navel and she wasn't wearing a bra – I could see the outline of her breasts and the dark skin around the nipple area. I would be lying if I said I wasn't feeling turned on.

I tried not to stare. I did. When I forced my gaze from Robyn's body and looked up, she was staring me dead in the eyes. My eyes darted from left to right, up and down—I didn't know where I was supposed to look.

'Sorry. I didn't mean, I wasn't—' I said, a mouth full of alphabet soup.

'It's okay, I don't mind,' said Robyn. 'I actually kinda like you looking at me like that. You see me, I've never had that before.'

She took a step forward and pushed her body against mine; forcing me back against a tree, staring me in the eyes the whole time. I cold feel her breath on my face, her lips only millimetres from mine. I could smell the bubblegum ice cream.

She took my right hand in hers and slowly guided me, placing my hand on her left breast. The rhythm of her heart picked up pace as I touched her, and she let out a feeble gasp.

I pulled Robyn even closer with my free hand, embracing the scene with not a care in the world – I wouldn't have noticed if the world exploded in that moment. I was lost in her.

Wires broke free from Robyn's body, piercing her

skin as they escaped, and danced all the way into my heart, jacking into my soul, charging me up. Her eyes turned to silver, ghost-like, no pupils, and her lips a pastel shade of blue, rough and chalky. She whispered in my ear:

'Everything must die.'

The warmth of her delicate lips brought me back to life as she kissed me. Our very first kiss. A number of different emotions raved inside me. Things I'd never felt in my life before. A toxic fusion of love and violence, sadness and happiness, excitement and dread – all trying to take over me at the same time, stretching my psyche paper thin. All I could do was focus on the most important emotion and hope that it was victorious.

I focused on the happiness and, in my mind, I thought about it as a colour. Orange. Like a bag of Skittles, I separated all the orange ones into a single pile. And it worked.

I raised both hands and placed one on each side of Robyn's face, came back to life, and participated in the most beautiful scene of my life. We stood there kissing, like the way they do in the movies; we even had the wet hair, wet clothes, and were lost in the backdrop of lush, glistening trees. It was perfect.

I didn't want the kiss to end. I wanted to die right there in her arms.

I knew, as I stood there in the embrace, that my

likely cause of death was no longer suicide. I was now more likely to die of a broken heart. I could feel the love seeping into my veins like a fucking virus, tainting my thoughts in a horrible, pink, fluffy hue; sweet like candy floss, and it sickened me to my guts, but I liked it and wanted more.

I was already dead inside, so it didn't make much difference how I died in the end. I could taste the stench of Oblivion on the tip of Robyn's tongue, inviting me in, dragging me to Hell.

THE PARCEL

I forgot about the parcel in the back seat of my car until I was parked outside Robyn's house, dropping her off. We kissed and hugged a few times before she climbed out.

'Thank you for a lovely day, I had fun.'

'Me too, I can't wait to see you again.'

'Likewise, Love Cat. Open the parcel when you get home.'

Robyn blew a kiss, closed the door behind her, skipped away through her garden, and into her house. I watched her the whole way, hoping that she would turn around one more time before she went inside, and she did. She waved, then she was gone.

When I got home, I retrieved the parcel from the car and made my way inside. I set the parcel on the kitchen table and fixed Luna some food. She pranced in and out of my legs like she always did, and I bent over and scratched her behind the ear as she tucked into her dinner. I made myself some coffee and sat down at the kitchen table.

I couldn't remember the last time I received a birthday card, or a Christmas card, let alone a gift. I was excited to see what was inside. I untied the string and slid it off, tore the paper to reveal a painting on canvas. My heart jumped. Not with fear or dread, but with a sickening kind of happiness.

Robyn had painted a detailed portrait of me standing next to an old projector, arm leaning on the reel and all. She had captured me in such a light that I didn't recognise myself. I looked good. The painting was done in black and white with subtle hints of red and blue.

I sat there for a few minutes, admiring Robyn's art, before I felt the tears building up in my eyes. *You see me,* is what she said only a short time beforehand and, now I knew, Robyn could see me, too. I was hoping for a Kodachrome photograph to hang on my refrigerator, but the painting was so much better. I hung it on my living room wall. It still hangs there today.

Robyn turned up at my house that night, after I

sent her a message thanking her for the painting. She brought two bottles of wine, and pizza. We curled up on the sofa – Luna snuggled on Robyn's lap. We watched *Into the Wild.*

It was as if Robyn had been in my life for so much longer, like I had known her all my days. That got me thinking about soulmates, and a quote I once read in a magazine:

An invisible thread connects those who are destined to meet, regardless of time, place, and circumstance. The thread may stretch or tangle, but it will never break.

Ancient Chinese Proverb

Our first date was like the date that never ended. Robyn stayed over on Saturday, Sunday and, over time, her belongings gradually built up in my house – first it was a t-shirt, then a dress – and after two months, she had officially moved in with me. I somehow managed to net the girl of my dreams, and we were happy, truly happy.

However, happiness never lasts forever; there's always something lurking below, or hiding round the corner, waiting for the right time to strike.

The ocean is empty and the sharks are all here...

THE POET AND THE ARTIST II

There once was a poet and an artist. They fell madly in love. The Poet wrote endlessly, spilling ink over hundreds of pages – each sentence detailing the Artist's beauty in a new light. The Poet was broken, and this healed his mind.

The Artist worked on a never-ending portrait of the The Poet. With every single stroke of her brush, she pieced him back together again on canvas.

There once was a poet and an artist. They were broken, now complete.

HALLOWEEN

The vultures at The Box were sickened when they found out Robyn was my girlfriend, even more so when they heard about her moving in with me. Christie sniggered and whispered insults under her breath, and I murdered her in more violent ways than ever before.

The only person who was genuinely happy for us was Karen. She said that she knew we'd get on, and we did, we really did. We made a great team; we filled the gaping hole of loneliness in one another, after being infected for so long. I even cut my hair like Karen had suggested, got some new glasses, and was now sporting a full beard. I was looking good, healthy.

Robyn was cemented as an outcast. I felt bad about that, but she wasn't a bitter person and still tried to be a team player. Karen being Robyn's auntie, and a supervisor, was something that went well in her favour. Nobody wanted to lose their job over the situation, so most of the insults were aimed at me. I was used to it. I enjoyed the creativity of the insults, always evolving, never quite stabbing me in the heart.

There was a Halloween party that Friday night, and Robyn had been invited. I told her she should go, let her hair down, and have fun. Karen assured me that she would also be there for a couple of hours, so I didn't think Robyn would be left to wander around alone. I was never invited to any of the work parties because people assumed I wouldn't be interested and, to be fair, I never was.

Most work parties involve going *out,* but that was never the case at The Box. Instead, they had themed parties *in* the cinema after the final screening was over and the customers had went home—setting up tables and chairs in the foyer. They added vodka to the Ice Blast machines and people turned up with even more of their own booze.

Shut-in parties were illegal, considering the cinema didn't have an alcohol license at the time.

Even though I never went to any of the parties, I always felt like I had been right there, jigging with the parasites; people gossiped for weeks after, detailing the antics, who got off with who and all that kind of stuff. And then there was social media, another inescapable virus.

Deep down, I didn't want Robyn to have any part in it, but I also didn't want her to think I was a control freak, so I encouraged her to attend the party; something I would later regret. If there's one thing I've learned in life, it's to always trust your gut instinct. If something seems rotten, it most likely is.

My shift finished two hours later than Robyn's and, by the time I got home, she was already dressed -up for the party. She was wearing a white and navy nautical costume; striped with a red bow tied around the waist, white knee-high socks, and blue heels. As always, the outfit was topped off with Robyn's signature head scarf. She looked cute and I kind of wished there was no party.

'How do I look?' she twirled.

'You look great, sailor.'

'Are you sure you don't mind if I go? I can always stay home if you want me to?'

I could tell by Robyn's voice that she was looking

forward to going, and I certainly didn't want to be the old kill-joy.

'Not at all, you go and have fun. Please message me when you get there, okay? And let me know if you need a lift home.'

'I will do.'

And at that, a horn honked outside. Robyn gave me a kiss. The last real kiss I'd receive in a while.

'Have fun.' I said.

I secretly wanted it to be a terrible night so she'd come back to me—be careful what yo wish for.

Karen waved from the window as Robyn climbed into the car. I stood at my front door, watching as they drove away into the distance.

A new kind of anxiety fizzed in my stomach. I looked out at the bitter October night for a few moments longer, before heading back inside to put my feet up.

THE MESSAGE

Robyn didn't message me when she arrived at the party. I didn't worry too much because I knew she was with Karen. I was exhausted and fell asleep on the sofa. I would have slept there the whole night through but, at 2:16AM, my phone vibrated on the coffee table and startled me. Luna was asleep on my chest. I scared her to death when I bounced to life.

I knew something was wrong, even before I read the message. I could tell the message was rushed, and it just didn't sound like Robyn at all. There was a feeling of urgency in the words, panic even.

The message read: Plse come get me soon as you cn. I need out here!

I rammed my shoes on, grabbed my jacket, keys, and left.

The roads were clear, and I drove at 50MPH the whole way to The Box. When I arrived, a couple of people were standing around smoking outside, and then I noticed Robyn sitting down against the wall.

There was no time to fuck around looking for a parking space. I just stopped in the middle of the car park, got out, and jogged over to her like it was *The Bodygaurd*—take two.

She jumped up and threw her arms around me as soon as she noticed I had arrived to pick her up. I could tell she had been crying; her mascara was smudged around her eyes and she was still sniffling. I also noticed that the red bow tied around her waist was torn. My first thought was she had been in a fight of some kind.

'What the hell's happened, you okay?'

Her face was grazed, on her forehead, chin, and under one eye.

'I need out here, can just go?' she mumbled, the night capturing her vocabulary.

'Where is Karen?'

'Dave called, left early...a feel funny.'

She was sluggish, acting strange, and her eyes were rolling around like pinballs on downers.

The car was still running in the middle of the road. I ushered Robyn into the passenger side and helped her with her seat belt. She closed her eyes and was sleeping by the time we got home. I carried her into the house, up the stairs, and lay her on our bed.

'Robyn?' I said, shaking her. She groaned a few times and then nothing. She was dead to this world.

STUDY BUDDY

I didn't like keeping secrets from Robyn. She knew I was on medication for depression and anxiety – she was also on medication, so she could relate to that – but she had no idea I had Goat living in my study, or that he existed at all.

I went into the study at night and had full conversations with him, venting when I was angry, frustrated, bored, or if I couldn't sleep. Goat just sat there, looking at me with his little grey beard and that sinister smile. 'Everything must die' is all he ever said. I had come to believe he was programmed by some other force like a puppet. Or maybe I just made him up in my diseased mind.

It was hard to believe, only a couple of months back, I was terrified of the creature. Not any more, not at all; I figured, if he was sent here to claim my life and escort me to the hell I was destined for, he would have taken me already. I thought of him as a companion, a spirit guide, even. Whatever he was, he was no longer a foe. He's the only real friend I've ever had.

I couldn't sleep on the night of the Halloween party. I was worried about Robyn, hoping she was drunk, but there was something itching inside, telling me there was more to it than that. The only thing I could do was let her rest and find out what happened the night before when she woke up.

I made my way into the study and, as I had now come to expect, Goat was already there, waiting on me, leaning against my desk as though he knew my every move.

I sat down on the chair. Goat tapped his hoof on the desk. A flashback of him, clambering up the stairs when I was a child, streaked across my eyes in vulgar candy-cane stripes, settling back into the void in my memory a second later.

When I looked up, Goat had loaded a fresh piece of the old A4 into my my typewriter. He slammed his hoof on the desk and another flashback shot through my brain like cheese wire. When it passed I had the sudden urge to write. I hadn't bashed anything out in a number of weeks, not since I got together with Robyn, in fact. I cracked my fingers, and soon the keys were dancing in front of me as rows upon rows of fabulous words skipped along the page, and not only *one* page. By the time the burst of creative energy had faded, there was at least ten pages stacked neatly in a pile on my desk.

I was tired and could feel my eyes beginning to close over. Goat nodded. I stood up, made my way back to the bedroom. Robyn was still out cold, so I was careful not to disturb her as I climbed into bed. I gently put one arm around her and, soon after, I was trapped in an apocalyptic dreamscape with the beasts and the ghouls and the skunks and the demons.

THE MORNING AFTER
THE NIGHT BEFORE

I fixed Robyn breakfast in bed in the morning; bacon, eggs, toast, a glass of orange juice, and a black coffee with four sugars. When I made my way upstairs and into the room, she was already awake, sitting up in bed. She looked rough and confused.

'How the fuck did I get home last night? You pick me up?'

'Well, you sent me a text, remember? I think you had too much to drink.'

'Only had two drinks...I feel bloody disgusting. I can't remember texting you or anything.'

'Really? Are you sure you didn't drink more? You were pretty wasted when I got there.'

'No, two vodkas and that was it.'

She lowered her head, looked at the bow around her waist, and panic clicked in her eyes. Tears hugged her ducts for a second, then streamed down her face.

I set the breakfast tray on the bedside cabinet, sat down on the bed, and put my hand on Robyn's shoulder to comfort her.

'Hey, everything's okay. I promise you.'

'I think something bad happened last night. My mind is all foggy like one of those frustrating dreams you get...I feel sick to my stomach.'

She gagged, put her hand over her mouth, and cried. It was the first time Robyn had ever cried in front of me, she was breaking her heart. I leaned in closer, put my arms around her, and kissed her on the head.

'You remember anything at all?'

'I think...someone must have spiked my drink,

because I've had more to drink than that before, loads more. I've never felt this bad. There's blurry images flashing around in my head, but they don't make sense.'

'Let's piece it together. You left the house, got in the car with Karen, and then what happened?'

Robyn sat back against the headboard, put a hand on each temple of her head, and strained to put the jigsaw puzzle together in her mind.

'The first thing I remember is talking about *you* to Karen, I don't know what the conversation entailed, but she was laughing at me. There was music playing, crappy pop music. I had the window down.'

'I hope you were saying good things about me,' I tried to joke. Robyn didn't smile, she continued to strain her mind.

'So what happened when you got to The Box?'

'Red flashing neon lights, and cotton spider webs all over the walls. The music was loud and people were shouting to hear one another. We sat at a table in the corner with...Angus and Erin, and I think Angus poured me a drink. Karen had a Red Bull because she was driving. I remember her pinging the ring pull. We were all trying to chat over the music, it was blaring.'

'Is that all?'

'For fuck sake, give me a minute. I'm trying to

think...I remember something else.'

Robyn looked down and, still sniffling, picked the skin at the corners of her fingernails. I put my hands over hers to stop her picking her way to a bleeder.

'Tell me.'

'I...I...em, was alone with Angus in the office...and I remember him pulling at my dress. I slapped him. I think I must have passed out because there's a gap in time. When I came round, he was on top of me. The next thing I remember is sitting in the car park.'

The severity of what had happened dawned on Robyn, she put her arms around me and told me she was sorry, crying even harder. I held her tight, as tight as I could. My blood was boiling on the inside. I could feel the rage train chugging along my veins, but I had to stay calm for Robyn's sake.

'We need to go to the police and report that sick fuck, he's not getting away with this, not if I have anything to do with it. We need to do it now, before it's too late.'

I took out my phone and punched in *99*. Robyn snatched the phone from my hand before I could punch in the final 9 and hit *Call*.

'What the fuck?'

'What do you want me to do? I'll slit his fucking throat, I swear to God, I will.'

'Shut up and stop being stupid. I don't want anyone to know about this. I don't want the police. I just want to forget last night ever happened. I want it to go back to being you, me, and Luna. Can we please do that? I can't face the police, they'll make me out as a liar, and I don't think I can handle trying to prove otherwise. I can't *actually* remember what transpired in that room. Hardly a reliable witness.'

I ate the razors in my throat and tried to calm the racing thoughts in my head. I looked to my left. Goat was tucked up in bed next to Robyn.

Everything must die.

'What, we just let him do that and get away with it? You fucking serious?'

'What if he didn't do what we think he did? What if I've got it wrong? What then? He's got kids for fuck sake. All I know for certain is that *I* assaulted *him*.'

We sat in silence and, as I held Robyn, her tears warmed my shoulder. I could feel the pain vibrating through her body and, in that moment, she seemed much smaller than she was, more delicate.

Images of Angus on top of Robyn flashed through my mind, attacking my every thought. I was glad I hadn't phoned the police, for I knew what had to be done. Angus tainted our perfect love in a single action and, to restore it, he had to die. Not just in my head. I had to end him in the real world.

PERFECT LOVE

I told Robyn I loved her in September – on her birthday. We had been going out for exactly a month. I'm sure I fell in love with Robyn the very first time I set eyes on her in Asda, but I never told her that.

We went to a carnival for her birthday. We ate candyfloss, held hands, went on the rides, stuffed our faces with popcorn, and I even won Robyn a huge stuffed unicorn. I know, such a cliché.

There was a roller coaster at the carnival called The Dragon King; the thing was intimidating, had six loops, and was apparently one of the fastest coasters in Europe at the time.

I didn't want to get on – I've never been a fan of roller coasters – but Robyn was excited to have a go, and she reminded me it *was* her birthday and all. I wasn't very good at saying no to the most beautiful girl in the world, so we stood in line.

An hour later everyone was scrambling for a seat. I didn't want to sit at the back, or at the front; of course, Robyn wanted to ride up front. She fired ahead to secure the seats and jumped in. I was nervous and had eaten way too much popcorn to be going on a ride of such calibre. I took my seat with a constipated grin on my face and wedged the unicorn between us. The unicorn taunted me with it's violet lips and pearl horn.

'You're not scared are you? Scaredy-cat.'

'Is it that obvious?'

'You have the cold look of fear in your peepers. Don't worry, I'll hold your hand. If we do somehow derail and die, we'll die together, right?'

'Right,' I said. 'That's a comforting thought.'

The ride gasped to life and chugged its way to the top; every mechanical *click* made me jump. *Click-click-click*, like a metronome dancing in time to our inevitable doom.

As we reached the top, right before the first huge dip, I turned to Robyn and said:

'I just want you to know, if we die, I'll die happy, because at least I got to love you.'

Robyn's face lit up and her pale cheeks glowed.

'I love you too!' she screamed as we fell from the sky.

We were lovers in flight, gliding through time. A memory that would last for eternity. A flawless image of perfect love. The world was upside down and side to side all at once and, after a few moments, I had no idea what was up and what was down. My stomach was in my throat, then in my shoes, and I was sure I was about to blow chunks – thankfully I didn't. I could hear the laughter of children from below, the sound of the arcade, and I could smell the beauty of the world as the bright lights glimmered in our eyes.

The ride finally came to a halt without anyone dying. I was dizzy and felt sick, but I was laughing because I enjoyed the ride a lot more than I thought I would.

'You alright there? You look ill.' Robyn said.

'I'm fine and dandy.'

We spent the rest of the night strolling, holding hands, talking, kissing, excited about life. We couldn't quite believe our luck, finding each other and all.

If I could go back to that day, I would go back a million times over. Life had finally dealt me a winning hand in a poker game full of shitty cards.

SURVEILLANCE

Robyn quit her job after what happened at the Halloween party. Karen was surprised. When she asked why, Robyn said she wanted to concentrate on her art. Karen was proud of her, and even encouraged her to chase her dream of being a full-time artist—I wonder what she would have said if she knew the truth.

Anyway, I went to work on Sunday and acted as if nothing had happened the night before. When I arrived the cobwebs were still hanging on the walls, and the place didn't feel the same – the sight of the place sickened me. Everything from the posters, to the syrup seeping from the Coca Cola machines.

When I saw Angus that day the hairs on the back of my neck stood up, and I wanted to cut his throat right there on the spot, witnesses and all – but I knew I had to be smart about the situation, didn't want to draw attention to myself. No, I played along with the whole charade. The worst thing was, the bastard thought he was getting away with it, and was his old usual self with me. *Not this time, Angus boy,* I thought. *Not this time.*

I was like a zombie and I couldn't think straight. The only thing I could concentrate on was the multiple possible ways to kill Angus. I wanted to slice his throat open and gut him like a pig, but that would have been too quick and I wanted him to suffer.

Burning him alive was a good option, but I figured it could cause too much of a scene – the last thing I needed was some fucking rubbernecker crashing my party and calling the fire brigade. The game would be up if that happened.

I knew I was going to slaughter Angus in one way or another, but I didn't want to end up in prison serving a life sentence for murder, that just wouldn't do at all. I couldn't leave the love of my life out here all alone, so I would need to make a solid plan before I done anything else. And what better way to start a plan than by doing a little surveillance? It's the best way to observe the victim's behaviour, their comings and goings.

When my shift ended, I waited in my Jeep in the car park, never taking my eyes away from the main entrance. The automatic doors opened and closed at least twelve times a minute; mainly from customers going in and out – every now and then an employee would come out for a sly cigarette. I knew Angus was still in there. I made sure he was before I left.

I thought the bastard was never going to leave, but he finally did—two and a half hours after my shift ended. Game on.

As I watched him walking to his car, I figured all the rumours were probably true and, for a split second, I thought about what he had put Christy through, the abortion and all.

A whole new light was hanging over Angus, it didn't paint him well. He was more puny, pathetic, and unremarkable than I'd ever imagined he was – he looked small and insignificant as he made his way to his car.

He was almost bald and had an attractive wife and kind children he didn't deserve to have, and they didn't deserve to have him as a husband and father. I thought a lot about his children. Would they grow up broken, or would they be happy when the police knocked on the door and notified them Angus had been found dead?

He climbed into his car – a red BMW M3 – and drove away. I started my engine, let a few cars get behind him to shield my presence, then followed him home.

Angus lived in a big house, not as fancy as Robyn's family home, but substantial enough, in a nice part of town. I tailed him until he indicated left. I pulled in as he continued into his driveway. He climbed out and his car beeped and flashed a second later, and then he was gone.

Was he away to make love to his wife, kiss his children goodnight, or masturbate over the criminal images stored in his head? I couldn't be certain, but I wondered. I wondered what his bedroom looked like. Egyptian cotton sheets to keep him cosy at night? Perhaps. I thought about a lot of things when I was sat there in my car. *How does he take his coffee in the morning? What's his favourite show? Is any part of his life worth saving?*

I pulled out a notepad from the glovebox, rustled around until I found a pen that hadn't dried up on me. I jotted down his house number on a fresh page, 77, and his car registration, AR GU5.

I followed Angus home for a few days, scoping him out. If I'm honest, I enjoyed the game. I liked how he thought his secret was safe, that he was getting off scot-free. In reality, there was a young man outside plotting against him. Angus was able to pay Christy off, but I wasn't so easy. No price would do, even if he flashed a million bucks my way.

My mind was set. I often question my actions, and if I am just as bad as him. Someone would have ended up dead along the line, anyway. That much I'm certain of. Angus just happened to give me a great excuse to act out my debaucherous fantasy, once and for all.

On the fourth night of creeping around, I pulled out the notepad once again and worked on my plan. I was taller than Angus, and I figured he wouldn't be too hard to subdue and kidnap, but I had to be certain he didn't over power me, that would be embarrassing.

I scribbled down the ideas running wild in my head. After an hour of straining my brain I had formulated a plan. I played the whole scenario out in my mind multiple times, and I'd be lying if I said there was no selfish, perverse gratification in doing so.

Goat was by my side the whole time, cheering me on, marvelling in my devious plan. He nodded every now and again with approval.

I played out the news report in my head; the police appealing for witnesses, Angus' distraught wife balling her eyes out on the six o'clock news, Fiona Bruce informing the world about the search for the wonderful husband, father, rapist.

MELANCHOLY MONOCHROME

Robyn looked like death. Her ribs were visible and her face was gaunt, skin pale, almost blue, hugging to her jawline for dear life. I was useless. I tried my hardest to reconnect with her, but he was gone – mentally dead and physically dying.

Her days were spent in the study, which was now a shared space. All I needed was a desk and my typewriter, so I pushed my desk up into the corner to give Robyn the majority of the room, creating a mini painting studio.

Goat still lived there, surrounded by a million shades of melancholy monochrome, but he was invisible and took up no space at all. He'd spend just as much time in there as Robyn, admiring her work.

She painted all through the night and slept all day. I longed to feel her close to me. It would take time. I prayed once again, to all the gods I don't believe in, to save her from pain. *Take me instead*, I pleaded. *Burn me on the cross. I give myself as a sacrifice.* They didn't listen, and I wasn't surprised.

The paintings were haunting, full of suffering

and dismay, a far cry from the refined portrait of me. Sometimes I stood by the door and listened. I could hear paint splashing, Robyn grunting, and loud music booming from the speakers – she had taken a liking to Black Rebel Motorcycle Club. On repeat.

NOVEMBER RAIN

Days melted away like candle wax, dripping into weeks, canvas after canvas piling up against the wall, slowly closing Robyn off from existence. I went to work, came home and just sat in the living room watching the November rain rolling down the windows. Luna, my saviour, was never far from my side. Usually I would watch a movie to occupy my mind when I was lonely. That was no longer the case. Instead I dreamed of murder, tainting the rain red. Everything changed in the second week of December.

FAREWELL

I heard her bones crunching as her fragile body was dragged along the pot-holed road. My own bones were vibrating with shock.

The driver was speeding away by the time I got to the end of the street. The car registration was a flash of yellow and black. I memorised the first four digits before it was lost in a frenzied blur of death and destruction – M713.

The car was a banger of a Vauxhall Cavalier, an oily green colour with one red door. A rust bucket that shouldn't have been on the road in the first place, making her untimely death all the more painful.

I was wearing nothing but boxers. I didn't care. I wanted her to know I was there, that I would love her forever, that I would find her in the next life and lover her there again, maybe even more than I did in this life.

I cradled what was left of her head, brains and blood dripping through my fingers. I was amazed when I felt her chest and she was still breathing. I pushed my face close to hers, so that she could feel me, so that she wasn't alone in death. She looked at me with her marvelous marble eyes. *Its okay*, they whispered. *Its okay. Time to go.* She smiled before she drifted off into the darkness. I swear, she did.

Her fur was stained red, just like it was on the night she saved me from suicide. Luna had been my friend, my confidant, my partner in crime. And now, some bastard had put her in the ground before her time was up. There was no justice in it. None at all.

I had went outside to puff a smoke and feel the air on my naked skin. I was careless and left the door open wide enough for Luna to escape into the night. It was an honest mistake, but it cost us all dearly. Something I would never forgive myself for.

Robyn ran to the road – the most I had witnessed her moving in weeks – and put her arms around me. We cried together over our dearly departed Luna like a couple of crazy people, and maybe we were, but we had lost the third member of our family, and it branded our souls forever.

COUNTDOWN TO MURDER

I spent a lot of time driving around the city with Goat after Luna died. The anger I had inside of me was stronger than ever before. Reality was blurring into fantasy to the point that, on occasion, I couldn't tell the difference.

Nothing ever changes in the city. The same kind of people litter the streets and feed off the night like rats, plaguing the bars and alleyways. I wanted to end them all, to massacre every last one of them until the city was silent and calm.

Every thought inside my head was a violent one, I was losing myself and, sometimes, I had no other emotion besides the furious rage burning my gut. I needed it to stop before it consumed me beyond recovery.

I couldn't sleep the night before the murder. My mind was too active and I was anxious. I couldn't stop thinking about the aftermath. I was terrified of losing Robyn, more terrified than I was of losing myself. I couldn't just dip my toes in, however, for once I was in, I was in. No way out.

You've been a loser your whole life, do you really think you have the guts to go through with this? You'll fuck it up. You fuck everything up. You couldn't even look after a cat. The voice nagging in my mind tortured me at every turn, taunting me.

I was awake all night, alone, watching the darkness fade to navy, to a cool blue, and when the first ray of sunshine climbed in through my window, I got out of bed and got dressed. 7:00AM.

I popped my head into the studio and Robyn had fallen asleep against the wall, her knees tucked up to her chest, her head resting on her knees. I didn't wake her. She looked a little uncomfortable, but at least she was sleeping. I blew her a kiss and whispered 'love you,' then made my way downstairs and out the door.

ABANDONED UNDERWEAR
AND TINDERBOX GIRL

Most shops don't open in Glasgow until 10:00 AM on a Sunday, some later than others, so I walked around aimlessly in the crisp morning air. The usual signs of a wild night before were scattered around the streets – takeaway cartons, beer cans, smashed bottles. I even encountered a pair of skimpy female underwear and a single Nike trainer.

I can understand the underwear. An alfresco fuck session can easily lead to a person losing their scants. The trainer, on the other hand, I find bizarre. Does that mean someone walked home with only one trainer on? And I see this quite a lot, single trainers scattered around the city.

Some people can't afford new trainers. I like the thought of a homeless guy finding two discarded trainers, on separate occasions, that match. It would feel like winning the sportswear lottery to someone down on their luck like that.

The scent of vomit and urine is most prominent in Glasgow on a weekend morning but, when I channelled it out of my nostrils, I could smell the smokey scent of morning coffee.

The closest coffee shop was Tinderbox, so I made my way there to see if they were open for business, and they were. I went inside and waited at the counter to be served.

Tinderbox was dead, only one girl in the corner hugging a warm brew with both hands, a lipstick stained pout, and panda eyes. *Rough night.*

A young guy appeared from the back to serve me. I ordered an Americano, two sugars. Five minutes later I was sitting at a table with my drink, killing time. I took a seat close to the harlot of the night, just so I could observe her.

Under the night-old lipstick and mascara, there was a pretty face in hiding. Her hair was long, poker straight, and brown. Her outfit, however, was a bit much. She was wearing a dress – if you could call it that – with an elongated V, which danced so far as her belly button. And the bottom half wasn't any better – revealing would be an understatement. She wasn't wearing any tights, or shoes for that matter. Her shoes were on the table, blue wedges. I cringed a little. My mother used to say it was bad luck to place shoes on the table.

'You got a problem?' She snarled. I looked up and she was burning a hole in my face with her eyes.

'Me? No problem at all, just drinking my coffee.'

'Why you staring at me then? You a mad pervert or summit?'

The balls on this one.

'I can assure you I'm not a pervert.'

'You like what you see?'

'Well, I mean—'

'Cat got your tongue, aye?'

She smiled. Her teeth were too white to be real.

'Only joking. You were proper staring at me though, was freaking me out.'

'Sorry, it's a bad habit.' I said.

The girl got to her feet, picked up her shoes and mug, walked over to my table, and sat down.

'Nah, I'm just being a snappy bitch. I had, like, the worst night ever. I've been a dirty stop-out.'

'Why is that, out partying all night?'

'It was a party but everyone started arguing so I went home with this grotty dude.'

She slapped her hand to her head.

'My nut is bloody bangin.'

'Doesn't sound too good. What was the arguing about?'

'There's this girl, Lisa. She got off with my friend Celine's boyfriend Connor the other week. Celine found out last night and lost her shit. And then this other girl Susan got involved, and it turns out she got with Connor as well. He's such a player, but I told Celine that before she got with him, but she wouldn't listen to me, so it's her own fault. It was frying my nut though.'

'Sounds like you had a more eventful evening than I did.' I said.

My eyes were fixated on her jugular. Her skin was tanned, her neck thin. I crawled over the table, pulled her head back, and bit into her clavicle, my teeth sinking into her flesh like a knife to butter. The blood was bitter and oily on my tongue.

'Are you okay?' the girl asked, clicking her fingers. I snapped back.

'Yeah, sorry, I zoned out a bit there. I've not been sleeping.'

'Aww. Anyway, this guy David, he's been trying to get me back to his for ages and after a few drinks and a few smarties it seemed like a good idea. Got back to his flat and it was a total dump. And he was all over me. Total melt of a guy.'

I pushed her hands back and got on top of her, continued sucking the blood from her throat.

'Why is everyone called Dave or David these days?'

'What? You're kind of a weird guy, aren't you? A bit of a space cadet, eh?'

'Seriously, I know so many fucking Daves.'

'Maybe it's just a popular name? I know loads of people called David, and Douglas, so many guys called Douglas. What's your name?'

'Fre—Frank. My name's Frank, you?'

'That's such an old guy name. Sorry, but it is.'

'I'm not even thirty yet.' I joked. 'What's your name?'

'Elise. Does it suit me?' she said, whipping her hair back and putting her hands up like Marilyn Monroe.

The name didn't suit her at all. Elise is a classy name, but this Elise was a bit mental and less than classy. Or maybe I jut got her on a bad day.

'Yeah, it does actually suit you. I like it.'

'Aww, thank you. You're actually kinda cute.'

Shit. You can't be getting turned on, not now, get yourself together, man.

'You're not bad yourself.'

Goat popped up in the chair next to her and slapped his commanding hoof on the table.

'Thanks...So you fancy drinking up and getting outta here?'

'Eh, I would. But I've got so much on at the minute.'

'That's a shame. I like the strange ones, know? Why don't you put your number in my phone and we can meet up another time when you're free?'

I stuck my hunting knife into her belly button and dragged it all the way up to her throat, connecting the dots with the bite marks. I made a mental note to find my knife when I got home.

'Sure.' I said.

I took her phone and bashed in my real number,

not a fake one like I should've done.

'Thanks. Talk soon, Frank.'

She stood up and walked out the door. I wanted to follow the rough-round-the-edges Elise, pull her down a side street, fuck her from behind, and plunge a blade into what was left of her soul. But I didn't. I watched her leaving and sipped the last of my coffee. I ordered another one. After my second coffee, I left.

IF I HAD A HAMMER,
I'D HAMMER IN THE MORNING

I didn't want to buy my full kill kit from a single shop that day in case it looked too suspicious, so I shopped around a number of different stores. We Won't name them.. My list was as follows:

Tape
Surgical gloves
Bin liners—lots of bin liners
Safety goggles
Balaclava
Dust mask
Boiler suit
Boots
A fresh pillow case
A huge set of steel balls
Courage

When I was browsing one shop, I happened to walk down an aisle full of beautiful hammers: Mallets, sledgehammers, ball-pein hammers, every single type of hammer you would ever need. My eyes, however, were attracted to the stunning array of claw hammers.

I picked a few up to feel them on for size. Too big, too heavy, too small, and then I found the perfect swinger. The handle was a deep burgundy colour. The neck was short, the claws sharp. I ran my fingers across the claw and admired the blunt side, round like a steel cherry. I could feel it smashing into bone. A must-have killing implement. I added it to my basket and continued on my way.

If I got caught on my first kill, I wanted to make sure it was a good one. I wanted to be like Joe Pesci, De Niro, Alex DeFucking Large. I wanted Scorsese to take note and make a film about me.

They'd say I was the real life Travis Bickle, cleaning up the streets, ridding the place of scum. Prison wouldn't be as bad if I was infamous. But I pushed the thought from my mind. I had Robyn to think about. I was a great liar, and I knew I could do it without raising any suspicions.

I often thought about asking Robyn if she would like to participate, which would have been a risky move. *What if she freaked out and went to the police? What if she thought I was a psycho and stopped loving me.* We couldn't have that. I kept it all to myself. How hard could it be, living a double life? I'd pretty much been doing it all my days.

A LUCKY DEVELOPMENT

I planned on making Robyn some lunch when I got home. When I walked into the house there was a small suitcase at the bottom of the stairs. My heart sank, she was leaving me.

'Robyn?'

The kettle clicked in the background. I walked into the kitchen and she was pouring a cup of tea.

'Hey,' she said, kinda chirpy. 'You want a cup of tea or coffee?'

'Coffee would be nice, thanks. What's going on? Why the suitcase?'

'I told Karen I was feeling down, so she said we should get away. She's taken a few days off and is going to drive us up to Skye. You don't mind if I go, do you? I know it's short notice, but I think it's just what I need.'

My stomach danced in relief.

'I thought you were leaving me...like, just when I saw the case.'

She walked over and put her hands on my face.

'Of course not, silly. You're my knight in shining armour.'

She kissed me on the mouth. The first kiss in a while. She was a little manic, too happy.

'You know I love you, right? No matter what happens, I'll always love you?'

Robyn put her arms around me and whispered in my ear,

'And I'll love you forever, in this world and the next.'

My biggest obstacle had now been removed. I was trying to figure out an excuse for being away during the night and, for the life of me, I couldn't find one. Robyn had just answered my prayers.

I went upstairs, sat down at my desk, and typed out a letter to Robyn. It read—

'Freddy, Karen is outside. I'm going to have to go now.'

I ran down the stairs.

'Sorry. Here, take this. Don't read it until you get there, promise?' I said, handing over the letter.

'Promise. I'll read it before bed. You're such a sap.'

I helped Robyn out to the car with her case and, as Karen waved, I had a flash back to Halloween night – it was the exact same setting. This time I signalled for Karen to roll down the window, and she did.

'Sorry for stealing your girl.'

'Just make sure she's okay, please?'

'Of course I will, don't worry. We'll take loads of snaps so you can see.' Karen leaned forward and whispered, 'I think it's lady problems.'

If only you knew the truth.

Robyn got in the passenger side and pulled on her seat belt. She leaned forward and slid a disk into the player.

'sixteen, my love.'

She winked. I smiled. Karen was confused,

'You guys are too cute.'

THE WAITING GAME

3:00PM. The clock blinked, my legs twitched. I put my hand down to pet Luna. She wasn't there. I played music, New Order. 6:00PM. Time dragged. Angus was finishing at 10:00PM.

I poured myself a whiskey. And another. I pulled out a rucksack and filled it with the gear. An Idea scrambled to my mind just then—*What if I leave footprints?*

I walked into my room, determined to find my hunting knife. It didn't take long. I was halfway under my bed, feeling around, when a box met my hands. I pulled it from under the bed. The box was black, tattered, and torn. I removed the lid, unsure of what was waiting for me inside.

On top of the pile inside the box, I found pictures of my mum. She looked happy. There was one of her at my birthday party, forcing a smile. Only now could I identify the sadness on her face. I didn't want the pictures to weaken my heart, so I flipped them over to the white side and, under the photographs, I found my hunting knife. It was waiting there to be found the whole time, unsheathed and everything. I picked up the blade and cut through the air a few times. I slid the knife down the tip of my thumb and it cut into me with ease. I pulled my thumb away and sucked the blood, a mouthful or iron.

I took the new black boots to the living room, knife in hand, flipped them over, and began cutting random shapes from the rubber. I wrapped up the rubber shavings in newspaper and set them alight in a bowl, then flushed the ash down the toilet.

7:00PM. I had some Scotch and a cigarette to calm the old nerves. 8:00PM – another cigarette and a bottle of beer. This went on for a while. I watched the clock the whole time, to the point it seemed like the world had malfunctioned and was stuck in the same gear. I listened to Black Rebel Motorcycle Club, and a bit of Nirvana's Bleach. 8:32PM – time to rock.

DRESS UP

I went to the bathroom and pulled on the navy boiler suit – it was a snug fit. I put on the boots and proceeded to wrap my ankles with silver tape. I slid my hands into a pair of powdered surgical gloves and taped around the wrists—this was a tricky task. After I had pulled on the balaclava, goggles, and dust mask, I checked myself out in the mirror.

When I was convinced I looked the part, I took off the goggles and dust mask, and rolled up the balaclava to look like a beanie. I spent another few minutes looking in the mirror, building up courage, slashing the air with with my knife, before putting it in my pocket, going down stairs, and out the door to the car.

I lined the boot of my Jeep with a double layer of bin bags, secured with enough tape to hold the plastic in place, then jumped in the driver's side, placing my rucksack of devious goodies on the floor of the passenger side.

When I started the engine I looked at my simple house, and had the horrible feeling that it would be the last time I'd ever see it.

For the first time in years my dad's voice rattled in my brain, 'I bet you're just a little faggot.' My eyes were burning. *Now or never.* I slammed my foot on the accelerator.

HAMMER TIME

I arrived at Angus' street at 9:38PM. I was too early, so I parked at the end of the street, shut down the engine, and waited. Every car that pulled into the street was a potential victim, because I found it hard to see the cars and the people in the darkness.

I wanted to be sick. My hands were sweating inside the gloves and, for a second, I lost my nerve. I thought about Angus on top of Robyn, and that was all the inspiration I needed to get my shit together.

I reached over to the passenger side, opened my bag, and slid out my new hammer, spun it around a few timed in my hands. I then pulled out the pillow case and tape, laying both on my lap. I was a surgeon of justice preparing for a big operation, everything splayed out in front of me.

My heart was thumping. My breathing was fast and erratic. Goat was in the back seat with an excited grin on his face. He placed his hoof on my shoulder, and it calmed me. I had to focus hard to control my breathing. A minute passed and I was breathing like a monk. Even the anxiety had eased off, although my hands were still shaking.

10:00PM came and went. No sign of Angus. The Box was one of those unpredictable jobs where anything could happen, resulting in being held back for a number of different reasons. I knew this from my own experience.

My shifts always ran at least thirty minutes over. One night I was held back for an extra three hours, which I didn't get paid for, but it was Karen who needed my help. She was always nice to me, so I didn't mind.

Angus swerved into the street with full beams at 11:11PM. I clenched my sweating fist around the hammer in my right hand. I slid the balaclava down over my face, secured the goggles, and adjusted the dust mask. I then stuffed the pillow case into my back pocket and slinked out the door with the tape in my free hand. I left the door open and made my way over to Angus' car. I crouched a few metres from his BMW, waited until he climbed out and, after the *beep beep*, shot forward.

11:11

Some people believe the number 11:11 has a kind of powerful significance. The numbers added together accumulate to four. The number four is something I can't quite explain, but it has always been stuck in my head, and I like multiples of it. The fascination took hold of me the night my mother died. I'd bite my tongue a certain way, four times. I'd switch the lights on and off each night, four times. I'd clench my teeth together in multiples of four, imaginary floating squares dancing around my head in groups, until I reached sixty-four—and then I'd start again. I call it counting sheep for weirdos. If you've been paying attention to this story you will find evidence of my obsession: four, eight, sixteen, thirty-two. Thirty-two is the most perfect number combination on this planet.

Some believe 11:11 is a sign that angelic beings are in close proximity. That they come with love and protection, bringing clarity and guidance. 11:11 is the number of masters. Said masters are sending a message that you, yourself, are a divine aspect of the Universe – a master of forward thinking, and truly becoming who you were supposed to become. It all made sense to me as I charged towards Angus. It all made sense.

KILLING TIME

I still experience the horrendous crunch of hammer to bone when I close my eyes each night. I was expecting a lot of screaming and struggling, but one swift strike to the back of Angus' head rendered him unconscious. He fell to the ground instantly, blood pissing out all over me, one leg twitching. The adrenaline shot through my veins in abundance. Goat was standing there cheering me on the whole time.

I pulled the pillow case from my pocket, rammed it over his head like a hood, and taped it at the bottom. I then taped his hands, crossed behind his back, and another helping of tape around the old ankles.

I was surprised at how strenuous it was to move an unconscious body. (Trust me, think about this aspect before you decide to murder someone, it's something you may overlook, like me, but it's an important factor to consider.)

I heaved and heaved, dragging Angus away as swiftly as I could, but it felt as though I was dragging a meteorite across the surface of Mars. The only thing I could hear was my hammering heart, and a few times I could've sworn I heard police sirens. I was caught, for sure—but the cops never arrived. In fact, the whole world fell silent.

'Don't just stand there, grab his fucking legs!'

I barked at Goat and he complied. We bundled Angus into the boot. I slammed it over, climbed in, and got out of there, sticking to the speed limit as best I could.

A GAME OF TWO HALVES

Driving around with a body in the boot of your car will rip your nerves to shreds. I was expecting to be pulled over at every junction, jumped out my skin with every car that overtook us, and couldn't sit still when we were stopped by a red light. At one point a police car pulled up next to us at a roundabout. They hovered alongside us for too long, scoping us out, but they soon shot away in a flash of red and blue. I couldn't concentrate. Everything was like a dream, a neon blur of fictional madness—but it was all real.

I had removed the balaclava, dust mask, and goggles as we left Angus' street, but the sweat was still dripping from my face. The air-con didn't do much to help, so I rolled down the window to cool my burning skin.

I took the next exit to Oban, continued following the signs for the remainder of the journey. Goat had vanished by the time we reached our destination. I was expecting him to reappear at some point during the night, but he didn't. I was alone—well, almost.

I thought I was being paranoid when I first heard the thumping, but it happened on more than one occasion – short breaks of silence in between the outbursts of agony.

I pulled in at the old quarry from my childhood. Angus was banging around like King Kong on crystal meth. He was yelling like a teenage girl. I was unable to make out what he was trying to say as his voice was muffled, but he didn't sound too happy with his current situation, and I figured he was cursing me upside down.

I transported myself into the cramped boot, and to what Angus was thinking that night, as though I was the one being kidnapped and tied up.

All Angus knew at this stage was that he had been attacked, bound, and bundled into a car by a maniac. Every single person he'd ever wronged would be rattling around his head as he tried to figure out who was responsible for the living nightmare he was being subjected to.

I couldn't wait for the moment I pulled the hood from his head. *Surprise, motherfucker.* He would be shocked, confused and, maybe after a while, it would dawn on him how his actions a few weeks earlier had brought him face-to-face with the wrong guy.

THE CONFRONTATION

I was entranced by the fine haze of rain flickering like dust in the beam of my headlights. The lights created a yellow ring in the rubble, setting the scene. *And...action.* I sucked on a cigarette to calm my nerves, Angus still banging away in his temporary casket, before covering my face with the balaclava.

I walked over to the edge of the old quarry and looked down. I couldn't make out the water below, only darkness. I was staring into the eye of Oblivion, a gateway straight to Hell. I had the urge to dive in head first, but I had business to take care of, and it would have been selfish of me not to finish the job.

When I popped the boot, Angus had rolled over onto his belly and was trying his hand at performing the worm on the dance floor. He wasn't getting anywhere fast, and looked more like a fish out of water – panicking, struggling to save his sorry life. I punched him in the guts. He growled and wheezed.

'If you don't shut up I'm going to lock you in, douse the car in petrol, set it alight, and leave. Does that sound like fun to you? I swear, I'll do it.'

'What the fuck do you want?'

His voice tapered off in a high-pitched whimper. I punched him on the side of the head. A sharp, intense pain shot over my knuckles and through my hand to my wrist—I liked the thrill of it.

'Am I speaking Spanish? Shut your filthy trap.'

'Please, please, I'll be quiet.'

He was sniffling through mucus and tears.

'Here's what's going to happen. I'm going to ask you a question, and you're going to answer, okay?'

'Okay, just plea—'

Another gut punch, this time with my left hand to even out the pain.

'I can do this all night long. I'm going to ask you a question, and you're going to answer, okay?'

'Okay, okay.'

He gasped for air like he hadn't drained enough of the stuff already in his life.

'Good. Now let's get you out of there.'

Removing Angus from the car was so much easier than putting him in there. I grabbed his collar with one hand, the tape at his wrists with my other, the tape doubling up as a carry handle. When I pulled, Angus stretched out, pushing with his feet.

I hauled him to the front of the car, into the spotlight. The gravel helped his body glide over the volcanic ground as I steadied him up on his knees.

I was too warm, but shivering at the same time, the sweat cold on my skin. Dragging a man to his final destination was more of a workout than I had suspected it would be. I lit another cigarette and took a moment to catch my breath.

A million thoughts and ideas flashed around inside my head. The adrenaline pumping through my body was electric and filled me with euphoria, right to the very pore. I was tormenting a man, and I was enjoying every last second of it. I was a monster. That was no revelation to me. I had found my calling in life and I wasn't about to turn my back and walk away from such a gift.

I continued the interrogation.

'Do you know who I am?'

Angus tilted his head, registering my voice in his ears.

'I...I don't know.'

'Do. You. Know. Who I am?'

Angus was racking his brains underneath the hood. I could hear the wires in his head rattling around as he struggled to solve the Rubik's cube, hands-free.

'I do. I recognise your voice from...somewhere. What do you wa—'

I stomped my foot on his thigh.

'Fuck!'

'Stick to the questions.' I ordered. 'I'll give you a clue. *Would you like a drink with your popcorn?*'

'Holy shit. Fre...Freddy?'

I slow clapped, cheering as the penny dropped.

'Surprise.'

'You'll go down for this you crazy bastard. I

always knew there was something not right abou—'

A solid kick to the head knocked Angus to the ground. I pulled him back up to his knees.

'Not right about me? I could say the same about you, old boy.'

I snatched the hood from Angus' head to reveal a battered, swollen face. One of his eyes was almost closed. The other rolled around, adjusting to the bright lights. He gasped at the cool winter air. Old Angus was in a bad way.

'Now, I won't lie, this doesn't end well for you. But you still have some choices. We always have choices, Angus, decisions to make. You know about making decisions, don't you? You've made a few sick ones in your time.'

'What you going on about? I'm a family man, I work hard.'

'I wonder what your family would think if they found out about Christy?'

His head dropped.

'That was a long time ago, everyone makes mistakes. Is that what this is all about?'

'You know me. I'm not a fan of Christy, not in the slightest, but what kind of a man does that to a young girl? What if that was your daughter?'

'I'm sorry. I tried to fix it.'

'You'll be glad to know this has nothing to do with Christy. Like you said, that *was* a long time ago. It's all forgotten about now, right?'

'Look, end this madness, take me home, and I won't say a word. I'll say I got mugged. Won't even mention your name. I'll even promote you to supervisor, yeah?'

'If only it was that easy. Time isn't on your side, so here are your only two options. I'll give you a minute to think them over. One, you tell the truth and I'll let you walk over to the edge of that cliff there and you jump of your own accord. Option two, you continue to lie and I make you pray you had never met me.'

Self-pity escaped from the single wide eye on Angus' face.

'Please, you don't have to do this. I'll do anything you want, just don't kill me. It's almost Christmas and I've got kids.'

'Don't worry, I'll send your wife a lovely festive card.'

We often take life for granted. Always assume that there will be a next day, a next month, a next year, and a next Christmas. But that isn't always the case. You could walk out in front of a bus, a speeding car like poor Luna, die of cancer, or you could cross paths with your worst nightmare, someone like me, and end up murdered and disposed of like a bag of trash.

'I'm begging you. I've always been nice to you, Freddy, you know that.'

'Really? You can't honestly think I don't know what you did? That's hilarious.'

'I really can't!'

'I'll give you a hint. The Halloween party.'

I revealed the hunting knife from my pocket, passing it back and forth between my hands. There was a cold look of dread on Angus' face.

'Nothing happened, I swear. It's not what you think.'

'Strike one.'

I took a step forward and leaned down to meet Angus' face, placing the point of my knife on the left side of his forehead. I scraped the knife hard and deep with both hands, the flesh tugging as I scarred an *S* shape. The blood spewed out and I marvelled in my handy work. Angus was screaming and grunting the whole time.

'What do I think? Enlighten me?'

'Please. I don't know what she told you, but she's lying.'

'Strike two.'

'No, please stop!'

There was a gut-curdling scream as I added another letter, *C*.

'All you have to do is tell the truth and I'll stop.

What did you do to Robyn?'

'I swear, it was just flirting.'

I added *U* to the collection of slashes. The blood made the knife greasy in my hand, and the blade slid, making the *U* look like more of a *V*.

'Stop, fuck! I put some ketamine in her drink, but it was just a laugh.'

'Just a laugh. Do I look like I'm laughing? Was Robyn laughing, having a dandy old time was she?'

'You weren't even there. She was having a good time.'

I wiped the knife and my hands down the side of my legs to make sure I had a firmer grip as I added a final letter, *M*.

Angus looked like Carrie, however, he was acting more like Carrie from the shower scene than kick-ass Carrie covered in blood at the end of the film. He was blubbering and crying, and it was making me sick to my stomach. I stood back and admired my work of art on his forehead.

'Well ain't you pretty. S-C-U-M. It suits you. That's the trouble these days, there's too much scum clogging up society. You know what I mean?'

'You are fucking insane, just like your whore bitch! She wanted it, was begging me for it.'

His laughter cut through my brain with such intensity I thought my head was going to burst into smithereens.

My blood was bubbling and I couldn't think straight. I paced back and forth, figuring out my next move. Before I knew it I was lost in a frenzy of crimson fury.

The rage gave me god-like strength. Enough power to drag Angus to the edge of the cliff. I pulled him by the scruff of the neck with brute force like a caged beast, hungry for destruction.

Everything must die.

I dragged him to his feet, held his head, and stabbed him in the spine, at least eight times, before pulling his head back and slicing his throat in one clean cut.

Angus gargled his final breath of life, and he tried to say something, but it didn't materialise to much more than a dying man's mumble.

'Strike three, motherfucker.'

That was the final sentence Angus heard before I pushed him over the edge. Six seconds later, give or take, there was a splash, and he was gone forever.

The heavens opened and the fine, hazy rain soon became large marble-like drops, washing away the blood, the evil, cleansing the stench of death from the air.

AFTERMATH

I had finally done it. I didn't even feel bad – not a single shred of remorse in my body. Instead, a strange calmness washed over me like I had reached a state of nirvana. I had found a new drug. A drug better than anything I'd ever experienced in my life. An unprescribed elixir. I was addicted.

My body kicked into survival mode and all I could think about was getting away from the scene of the crime. I jogged over to my car, popped the boot, and undressed until I was completely naked. I put the clothes and everything on the plastic inside the boot. I then removed the tape I had used to keep the bin liners in place, and wrapped all the evidence inside.

From the passenger side of my car, I grabbed my bag, retrieved a change of clothes, and got dressed. My heart was thundering with the storm inside my chest, and I was beginning to shake. My head was vibrating in all different directions. My senses were heightened.

I took another bin liner from my rucksack and proceeded to secure the bundle of evidence inside, tying up my secret forever. All I had to do was get rid of the bag of evidence in a remote location on my way home.

When I climbed into my car and started the engine, I calmed down. I didn't recognise myself in the rare view mirror; there was a spark in my eyes, and I had a stupid grin on my face. I turned on the radio and pulled away in an orderly fashion.

HOME

I was elated when I stepped into my house. Everything was pleasing to me, as though I had returned home from a long, disastrous holiday. The scent in the air, the décor, the wooden flooring, the fucking kettle. I was delighted to be standing in my kitchen.

Something had shifted in me. I felt empty, but in a good way. Robyn was away with Karen. Luna was dead, and Goat, my tormentor, alter ego, guardian, had taken the night off. But I didn't feel lonely, and I wasn't depressed or suicidal. I was finally unchained from a lifelong nightmare of melancholy thoughts, feelings, and brutal flashbacks.

One thing I did feel, however, was a carnivorous hunger for bacon. And I was in luck—I had two packs in the refrigerator. I ripped into the plastic, poured some oil in a pan, and got the gas going. I savoured the smokey smell like it was the first time

I had ever experienced the scent of bacon in my nostrils. I brewed coffee, buttered some bread, and filled my belly with the thick, meaty sandwiches.

The time was 5.32AM. I finished my sandwiches, coffee, and smoked a cigarette, then made my way upstairs to get some sleep. I had work at 11.00AM.

The events of the night played out in my head, over and over again, but it didn't disturb me. I was replaying it in my head by choice, relishing every last detail. As far as first kills go, I done a good job. All I had to do now was act normal and avoid capture.

I closed my eyes after a while and drifted off. I had no nightmares. There was nothing but static bliss.

LATER THAT DAY

When I arrived at work later that day, my mind shot back to the first time I walked in through the automatic doors, all those years ago when I was kid. The infection had been eliminated – the air was now warm with the scent of freshly popped corn. Children played tag in the foyer, mothers stood in line with the hustle, bustle, and excitement.

My day was far from perfect though. Karen was away with Robyn, and Angus was—preoccupied, which meant Erin would be in her element – acting manager and all. I knocked on the office door and waited, and I just knew she would be in there watching me on the CCTV.

I was twenty minutes early. She was in there trying to think of something else to pull me up on, but there was nothing. She answered the door.

'Am I seeing things?' Erin said, prodding me in the stomach to make sure I was real. I played along with her game.

'New week, new me and all that.'

To my total disbelief, Erin smiled. She actually smiled.

'Well, let's see how long it lasts,' she said. 'Angus is a no-show today. He didn't even call in to let me know, so it's going to be a busy shift.'

'That's not like Angus, Mr Punctuality.'

'I know…either way, we'll need to work with what we've got. You might need to stay on a bit longer.'

'No worries.' I said, then made my way into the locker room to get ready to start my shift.

THE GOSSIP TRAIN

When Angus failed to turn up to work for three days in a row, people started whispering. The vultures got in line to board the gossip train, adding their own theories. Someone heard he had done the off with a younger woman, took the savings and everything and moved to Spain. Another person suggested he was depressed and just walked into the woods and killed himself. Endless theories.

I took a great amount of pleasure in knowing what had actually happened to Angus, and how he had met his end. For once, I knew something that the gossips didn't. I now had my own dark secret, and I planned on keeping it that way, taking it to my death bed.

A ROCK HEART

When I arrived home on Friday night the living room light was on – it was Robyn. I had never missed a living person so much in my entire life, and I couldn't wait to see her and put my arms around her.

When I walked in the front door I could smell something cooking. Robyn dashed out the kitchen and down the hallway to greet me. She jumped up into my arms, wrapping her legs around me, then planted kisses all over my face. Her lips were soft, and the flesh of her arms around my neck gave me shivers.

'I missed you.'

'I missed you too. Work went so slow today as well because I knew I was coming home to your pretty little face.'

'Aww.'

With Robyn still wrapped around my body, I hobble towards the kitchen.

'What are you cooking in there? Smells good.'

'I made you some nice winter soup to warm you up, it's getting so cold out.'

'That's sweet, thank you. Did you have a fun time when you were away?'

'Yeah, it was great. We stayed in this old cabin with a fire. We had lots of wine, talked a lot about girly stuff, and we even tried fishing...it didn't go too well.'

I was happy to see Robyn smiling again, with a genuine smile like she used to. She didn't seem as withdrawn as she was only a couple of weeks earlier. It would take time for her to heal, and she would never fully get over the trauma – depression and trauma has no overnight fix, I know from experience – but she was taking positive steps and, for that, I admired her. It's so easy to crawl down the rabbit hole, never to return.

'I'm glad you had a fun time...you'll need to fill me in on this fishing story though, because I have a funny picture in my head of how that might have played out.'

'Don't worry, I'll fill you in. Oh, I brought you something.'

Robyn climbed down and rustled around in her bag, then pulled out a plastic parcel. I opened it to reveal a small heart-shaped rock inside. she had painted the words 'SKYE LOVE YOU' on the rock. I didn't think it was possible for me to love Robyn any more that I already did, but in that moment, I fell in love with her all over again.

'You know I love you too, right? To the moon and back.'

'I do, I can see it in your eyes.'

'I'm glad you know that.'

'And I read your note every night before bed. It helped me sleep and made me feel safe."

MISSING

I sat down in front of the television and switched it on. Robyn brought in the soup and some buttered bread on a plate, salt and pepper. The soup she had made reminded me of coming home from school in the winter – thick, hearty. It hit the spot.

My heart sank when the news report flashed up on the screen. *The search for missing local man continues...* I changed the channel as quickly as I could, but Robyn had tensed up and asked me to switch back to the news.

The report was as follows:

A local man, Angus Riley, has been missing since Sunday night. CCTV footage shows Riley leaving his place of work in his car, but he failed to return home that night. His car was parked outside the family home and, for this reason, the police are treating his disappearance as suspicious. The police urge anyone who may have information regarding Riley's whereabouts to please contact the local authorities.

Robyn sat back and relaxed a little when the image of Angus faded away from the screen.

'How weird is that?' she said.

'Very weird.'

'Where do you think he is?'

I tortured him and stabbed him to death, then pushed him off a cliff to make sure. I'm a murderer, but I done it for you, for us.

'Beats me. I'm sure he'll turn up somewhere.'

'I know this is so wrong, but I kinda hope something horrible has happened to him. Does that make me an evil person?'

'Not at all. The guy was a scumbag. You don't have an evil bone in your body.'

'I don't ever want to see that man again. My skin is crawling after seeing his smug face again.'

'Trust me, my love, he will never be bothering you, or anyone else again. I promise.'

SECRETS ALWAYS
COME OUT IN THE END

They never did find the body of Angus, and the case is active to this day. However, after he was reported missing on the news, all his secrets emerged one by one – it was a sensational media frenzy. They ripped him apart and it turns out he was accused of assaulting three girls and one boy, all of which had been employees at The Box. The Troll backed him up, saying the accusations weren't fair, and that he wasn't around to defend himself. I often wonder if Erin knew more than she was letting on. I always felt as though Angus was too straight-edged. I knew there was something off about him from the first time I set eyes on him, it just took me a while to figure it out. Clean cut individuals tend to have the darkest secrets – people in power tend to have the same kind of lust for inappropriate behaviour.

MOVING ON UP

With Angus gone, there was a manager position up for grabs. I was certain it would go to Erin. It didn't. Karen was promoted from supervisor to manager. Erin was fuming. She left and, as far as I know, she is now a manager at our rival cinema, Cinecrooks.

The only thing I missed about The Troll was murdering her in my head every day. Although, after killing Angus, the glitches calmed down for a while and for some reason she didn't grind on my nerves so much.

I was happy to see Karen as the manager – she's the one who keeps the old motion pictures rolling, like me. She works hard and needs the money. She deserved the promotion.

With Karen as manager, her supervisor position had to be filled. Much to my disbelief, as I had no managerial or supervisor experience, Karen put me up for the job – and she gave it to me.

Being Robyn's boyfriend would have went well in my favour, but Karen always had a soft spot for me, and I for her, so that could've swayed her decision.

I was moving on up, no longer a bottom feeder like the other vultures. I was a king and they were my peasants. I'd be lying if I said I didn't enjoy the power, for I did, a hell of a lot. I had been set free from the chains of the sickening purple shirt and upgraded to a suit and tie.

Robyn was also moving up in the world in a different fashion. She was accepted into the Glasgow School of Art in January, 2013. I was making more money as a supervisor and encouraged her to focus on her studies without taking on a job on the side. Her talent had to be released into the world with no restraints holding her back from achieving the success she deserved.

We were settled and had managed to relax into an adult life together, working the grind and building a future. I even finished writing my very first novel, *Perfect Love*. And, of course, it was about Robyn. Life was dandy – for a time.

FLASHBACKS OF MURDER

On March 2nd, 2013, an old friend stopped by to visit. He was dressed in a dashing emerald-green suit, and was wearing a familiar smirk on his wiry face.

I was bashing away on my typewriter. I heard the rattling of hooves on wood. I got up out of my chair, opened the door, and there he was—my old friend Goat.

He sat on the desk like he always used to.

'I thought you were gone for good. I was getting worried about you, old boy.'

'Everything must die.'

I had forgotten those words, and the night of the murder was a jumbled mess of a memory. I'd almost convinced myself that it was all a dream, a figment of my imagination. But when those words seeped into my ears, my brain shocked into technicolour flashbacks of murder.

The urge for violence scraped at my psyche over the next couple of days or so, and it was too much to handle. The nightmares and the glitches shot back with a vengeance. Without even thinking about it, I was in my car, stalking the streets for my next victim.

The city street lights guided me on my quest for blood, neon images of violence projecting in 35mm film behind my eyes. The urge was taking me over. I needed to indulge in a bit of the old ultraviolence.

On the third night of scoping out a victim, I was desperate. That's when I had an idea. I took out my phone, flipped to my contact list, scrolled down, and hit *Call*. A voice buzzed in my lug a moment later.

'Hello.'

'Hi, Elise?'

'Who's this?'

'It's Frank, remember me?'

LOVE IS A HOWLING
BITCH FROM HELL

The Korova milkbar sold milk-plus, milk plus vellocet or synthemesc or drencrom, which is what we were drinking. This would sharpen you up and make you ready for a bit of the old ultraviolence.

Alex DeLarge,
A Clockwork Orange

Love is a howling bitch from Hell. Love drives us all mad. Love makes us do the craziest things. Things we would never normally dream of doing.

I realise now that these words were only ever an excuse. A way for me to justify my actions. I am a violent man. I am a monster. The beast hiding under your bed at night. I am the man at the bar. Standing in the coffee shop. The man holding hands with his girlfriend in the supermarket. I am the man standing next to you at the train station. The man standing next to you right this second. I am a walking virus. I am scum. I am a vulture. My name is Freddy Moon, and I *am* completely insane.

– Grant Jolly
June 16th 2018